SUSPICIOUS

SUSPICIOUS

BOOK FOUR IN THE ON THE RUN
INTERNATIONAL MYSTERIES

SARA ROSETT

McGuffin Ink

SUSPICIOUS
Book Four in the *On The Run International Mysteries* series

Copyright © 2014 by Sara Rosett

Second Paperback Edition: March 2017
First Paperback Edition: 2014

ISBN: 978-0-9982535-9-6

To the readers who asked for another Zoe story

"HAPPY ANNIVERSARY." JACK PLACED A large gift bag on the café table in front of Zoe.

She studied it then looked at him out of the corner of her eye. "I thought this trip was our anniversary present." She waved her hand, her gesture encompassing the tiny balcony where they sat, the pots of flowers spilling over the railing, and the buildings in pale yellow, faded pink, and ochre with their dark shutters that lined the street. She paused as a motor scooter zipped along the cobblestone street below them, its whine making conversation impossible. The drone of the scooter faded, and the distant sound of car horns from the busy street a few blocks away filtered back to them. The faint notes of Phil Collins singing about two hearts floated out of the open window of a nearby apartment. "You know, Rome."

Jack lounged back in his chair, which he'd positioned inside their hotel room, since the balcony wasn't large enough to hold two chairs and a table. He leaned forward, bringing his face close to hers, fastening his silvery blue gaze on hers. "You're not saying that you didn't get me anything, are you? Because I know you. I know you did."

Zoe raised her eyebrows. "But we agreed. This trip is expensive enough as it is." Even though a client of Jack's fledgling security consulting business had picked up the cost of their airfare and hotel for three nights, the other five days they'd tacked onto the trip purely for pleasure were coming out of their pocket.

Jack smiled slowly. "So, you did get me something else."

Zoe shifted in her chair, but didn't break eye contact. She didn't know if she could look away, even if she wanted to. She'd always been a sucker for those blue eyes. And when Jack gazed at her as he was now, with total concentration and a hint of a smile...well, it was a heady sensation. Of course, she'd never been one to shy away from situations that got her blood pumping. "I can neither confirm nor deny that."

In fact, she *had* gotten him a present, but there was no way she could bring it through airport security. The Glock was locked away in their house in Dallas.

"Very good. Nice delivery, no hesitation. If I didn't know you so well, I'd almost think that you were telling the truth."

"How do you know I'm not?"

"Because," he leaned closer, "your left eyebrow went up slightly higher than your right. It's your tell. You got me a present, too. And even if you didn't, I know you love surprises."

Her face broke into a smile. She closed the distance between them and kissed him. A girl can go only so long with those tempting lips millimeters from her own. She pulled back slightly. "I do love surprises. And, yes, I did get you a present, but you have to wait until we get home. Good thing you're patient."

"In that case, should we wait and open them together?" He reached for the bag.

She snatched it away. "No. You're the patient one, not me." She dug through the tissue paper while Jack settled back in his chair. She extracted a box about five inches square. She opened it and found another box. Inside was another smaller box. "Jack, this is crazy," she said, working her way through three more boxes, each one getting smaller. She loved every minute of it. Finally, she got to a square blue velvet box. It had to be jewelry. "Jack."

"Go on. Open it."

She pushed the lid back. Two square cut diamonds winked at her from a bed of pale blue silk. "Oh, Jack," she breathed. "You shouldn't have. You *really* shouldn't have."

"I wanted to," he said as he leaned forward to meet her kiss.

"They are beautiful. Gorgeous. But we can't afford these." Their budget was tight and certainly didn't run to diamonds. One year ago, they'd had an unexpected windfall when they recovered a valuable piece of stolen art, and received a finder's fee from the insurance company, Millbank and Proust Associates. They used the money to create Jack's company.

His background in covert operations provided plenty of experience, and the notoriety he'd received when the news broke about the recovery of the art helped them gain their first clients. After that first burst of interest, things had trailed off. They both knew that a new business didn't make money out of the gate, but it was going on one year, and Zoe could tell that Jack was worried. Zoe was used to stringing odd jobs together to make ends meet and had been able to boost their budget, mostly through her freelance copy editing of *Smart Travel's* guidebook series, but like many print publishers, *Smart Travel* had gone out of business. Zoe hadn't edited a guidebook in two months and had only had a few dog-walking gigs along with a smattering of virtual assistant jobs lately, so their bank account was pretty lean. The loss of the *Smart Travel* job was a sore spot, and she pushed her thoughts away from it.

He smiled easily. "Yes, we can." He took the box from her and removed the diamonds as he spoke. "I bartered."

She narrowed her eyes as her mind raced. "The Underwood account? You didn't give them a price break." Fixing the security system at an upscale Dallas mansion had been one of the few bright spots in Jack's schedule during the past few months, but Zoe remembered the final bill Jack sent them was lower than the estimate.

"The Underwoods were having a bit of a cash flow problem. They suggested paying the bill out over time. I countered with the barter suggestion. Mrs. Underwood was thrilled with the idea of getting rid of my bill with one of her 'trinkets.'" Jack handed her the earrings. "Go ahead."

She fastened them and went to look in the mirror over the dresser, pushing her hair behind her ears. "They're beautiful. Thank you."

Jack joined her. "You're welcome. He slid his fingers through the strands of her hair and gently twisted it away from one side of her neck. "Couldn't let our first anniversary go by without doing something special." He kissed her neck.

Zoe closed her eyes. "It's not our first anniversary." Their relationship history was...complicated, to say the least. They'd met and rushed into marriage, but the intoxicating haze of passion faded, and they found they were two very different personalities who seemed to clash over so many things. It was the worst time of Zoe's life—her hot, angry words thrown up against Jack's frosty silences had created an unbearable atmosphere.

They'd divorced, but couldn't sell the house they'd purchased. They'd compromised by living together in the house, but in separate areas. Remote roommates, they barely talked, communicating through notes and text messages. But then an issue in Jack's espionage past intruded, and their lives were never the same. It had taken quite a while, but they'd worked through their issues. Having married again, they were now a couple. But this time, without quite so much baggage and a commitment to work through whatever came their way.

"Isn't it?" Jack said.

She tilted her head as his kisses moved up her neck behind her ear. "I suppose it only makes sense to count our years as a married couple from the second wedding, the one where we got it right."

"Exactly," Jack said as Zoe turned in his arms to face him.

"I suggest we postpone our visit to the Pantheon," Jack said.

"We have been good little tourists, haven't we," Zoe said. "Not at all like last time." Last year, they'd spent their honeymoon in Rome. Jack had said afterward that except for a few excursions for gelato and pizza they might as well have been at home in Dallas. During this visit to Rome, they had actually seen some sites. Yesterday, they'd fought their way through the costumed gladiators and the aggressive tour guides to the rugged, but still impressive Colosseum, then they'd wandered among the fallen marble columns that littered the Forum. This morning, they'd trouped through the glory of the Vatican where so much of the marble stripped from the most ancient sites had been "recycled."

Zoe reached for the buttons on Jack's shirt. "Nothing will be open anyway. It's the siesta."

"Excellent idea."

Later, Zoe, who had been snuggled against Jack's bare shoulder, said, "You're sure about the diamonds?" She propped herself up on her elbow, thinking of the cost of the trip. They'd been eating cheaply and avoided souvenirs, but travel always costs more than the budget.

"No, Miss Tightwad. They're yours. Enjoy them. You need them for the opening."

Zoe looked at the midnight blue ball gown hanging on the closet door. "You're right. I hadn't thought about jewelry. Well, that's not true. I hadn't thought about my own jewelry."

The event that had brought them to Rome was tomorrow night, the invitation-only opening of a jewelry exhibit. The exhibit's sponsor was Millbank and Proust, which also insured several of the most valuable pieces. At Millbank and Proust's request, Safe Haven was providing extra security. Since Jack was the point man on the ins and outs of security and theft prevention, he'd focused his attention on the nitty-gritty details like the layout of the building and security cameras, which left Zoe free to pore over the catalogue of items on display, an array of gold and precious stones. Jack must have noticed her interest in the gems. She fingered the diamond earrings.

"Not in the same ballpark of what we'll see tomorrow," Jack said, sounding almost apologetic.

"But diamond collars and tiaras are so impractical. Can't wear them to the grocery store. The earrings are perfect." Zoe slipped on shorts and a sleeveless shirt. Rome was having an unexpectedly warm spring. "Have you gotten any more details about the opening?"

Jack shrugged. "Not much. It sounds like a typical gig."

"So what will you do?"

"Harrington hasn't briefed me on it yet. He said he'd get in touch today. I expect he'll call soon." Harrington Throckmorton worked for Millbank and Proust. They'd met the dapper little British man a year ago when he presented them with the finder's fee for the recovery of the stolen art. His company handled quite a few high profile objects, and while Jack hadn't said so aloud, Zoe knew that he hoped that this initial job with Millbank and Proust might develop into more work.

Zoe felt like she was beginning to figure out Jack. Her instinct was to throw most things out and discuss them to death, but Jack was more of an introvert and kept his worries to himself. During their first months together before their marriage disintegrated, she'd taken his silences as a withdrawal, a rejection, but now she realized that even though he hadn't verbalized his concerns, Safe Haven's sinking bank balance weighed on him.

Zoe looked at her gown. "Odd that Harrington wants me here, too. Sounds like that's something you could have done on your own—not that I'm complaining. I'm thrilled he wanted me to come to Rome, too."

"I suppose we'll be circulating, keeping an eye on things. He probably thinks a couple will blend in better."

Zoe pulled her hair into a ponytail then picked up their temporary cell phone they'd bought when they arrived in Rome. They didn't want to pile up outrageous international roaming charges, but Jack needed a phone, so a burner phone was the best solution. It was a basic phone, but it did have an email feature, which she opened and scanned. She couldn't ignore the tiny surge of relief she felt when she saw there were no new emails.

"Anything?" Jack sat down on the bed and put his shoes on.

"Nothing."

"You sound glad."

"I am." She plopped down on the bed beside him and took a deep breath. She'd been trying to ignore her feelings about her work—or lack of work to be more accurate—but she couldn't do it anymore, and they needed to talk. Approaching life as a team was still new to her, but she was getting better at it, and her feelings about her work were something she needed to talk with Jack about. It affected him, too.

"Look, this is going to sound weird, but I feel almost…relieved when I see there isn't a new copyediting job. I mean, I want something to turn up for the money aspect, but the copyediting part, not so much."

"So you don't want to do any more copyediting?"

"No, but it's more than that. I've been feeling…twitchy. You know how I am. I like the unknown, seeing what will pop up next, but lately I've felt dissatisfied, almost restless. I want to do something else, but don't know what."

"Do you want to go back to school? Get a degree?" Jack asked.

"Good grief, no," she said. "I was terrible at school. No, that's the problem. I want something different, but I don't know what it is. I've always loved drifting from one thing to another, not being locked in. You know, the 'let tomorrow take care of itself' philosophy, but now…" She hesitated, hardly able to believe what she was about to put into words. "Now, I think I want something more permanent." She threw herself back on the bed. "Listen to me. I'm turning all stodgy and conventional."

"Trust me, there is no way you'll ever be stodgy or conventional, no matter what kind of work you do. So you want a steadier job. Big deal. You'll still be you, eccentric and free-spirited."

"How can I be eccentric and free-spirited with an office job?"

"Who said anything about an office?"

"Because that's what I can do—edit, file, make spreadsheets." She ticked off all the things she did as a copy editor and as a virtual assistant. "The dog-walking gigs don't pay enough for me to do that full-time, but I'd rather scoop poop than sit at a desk all day."

Jack reached for her hand and pulled her up. "Plenty of jobs don't involve offices. I doubt you'll have to resort to full-time pooper-scooping."

"But I have no idea—literally *no idea* what else I could do."

"You don't have to make a decision today. Come on, let's get some dinner. You'll feel better after we eat. You'll figure it out."

"Okay," she said, making an effort to shake off the funk she was in. "We're in Rome. Can't do anything about it now."

She felt marginally better, having broached the subject with Jack. As they descended the stairs, she said, "You know, I can always count on your levelheadedness to balance out my bursts of freaking out. It's one thing I love about you."

"That's not exactly flattering, you know—that you love me for my levelheadedness."

"I said it was *one* of the things I love about you."

When they turned in their key at the front desk, the clerk handed Jack an envelope. "It's from Harrington."

"An old-fashioned note on paper, just his style," Zoe said.

Jack opened the folded paper. "He wants us to meet him at the Pantheon." He read the last line aloud, "Make sure you are not followed."

"I didn't think there was anything hush-hush about our being here or working with Harrington," Zoe said.

"I didn't either."

Zoe and Jack had left their hotel and walked several blocks to a bus stop then hopped off at the main train station, the Termini. They wound their way through the streets, passing vendors selling T-shirts, knock-off purses, and snow globes with miniature Colosseum replicas. They wedged themselves into a second bus then left that bus and walked a zigzag course to the Piazza della Rotunda.

"Finally," Zoe said, drawing in a breath. "We're good?" she asked with a quick glance over her shoulder at the narrow street they'd just walked. She hadn't seen anyone following them, but she had far less experience in that sort of thing than Jack did.

"Yep. Just us."

"Good." Zoe turned her attention to the view as she fanned herself with a map. It had been a long, sweaty trek. The snug piazza was completely different from the vast expanses around the Vatican. Five- and six-story buildings enclosed the space, their muted shades of taupe, buttery yellow, and even pastel blue tones glowed above the bright awnings and umbrellas of the cafés that ringed the piazza. Tourists meandered across the cobblestones to the Egyptian obelisk, the centerpiece of a fountain at the center of the square. "It's a different scale from the Vatican. Everything is smaller, even the obelisk," Zoe said.

"Wait until you see inside," Jack said, nodding toward the Pantheon, which made up one side of the square. "The outside is deceptive." Jack had visited Rome years ago when he worked for the American consulate in Naples.

"Oh, it looks so *complete*." Zoe grabbed his hand and threaded through the crowd, quickly moving across the cobblestones that sloped down to the Pantheon. The exterior was arranged in the classic Roman temple design with a triangular pediment and columned portico. "After the ruins of the Forum, I can't wait to see a Roman building with walls."

"The dome is nothing to sneeze at either."

"Amazing that you can't hardly see the dome from the outside," Zoe said. The pediment and hefty columns dominated the entrance. She'd edited several guidebooks about Rome and knew that it was the only building continuously in use as a place of worship—first as a temple to all the gods then later as a church, which saved it from the fate of looting and scavenging that the Colosseum and the Forum had suffered.

Zoe gently ran a hand along one of the massive 40-foot red

granite columns—more plunder from Egypt—that supported the portico, evidence that the ancient Roman builders either went big or went home. Then they were through the enormous doors and inside the cool hush of the church with its immense, coffered dome. Sunlight poured through the oculus, beaming down in a shaft of light to the intricately patterned marble floor.

"The size of it is overwhelming, even after the doors and the columns," Zoe whispered.

"I think it's something about the dome not being a huge part of the exterior design. It kind of takes you by surprise. It's one of my favorite places in Rome."

"Mine, too."

"You've said that about every place we've been."

"Can't help it. It's a fascinating city. I mean, where else in the world can you see a complete ancient temple, Egyptian obelisks, and have gelato, all in the space of a few steps?"

Jack opened his mouth to reply, but caught sight of something over her shoulder. "There's Harrington, by the tomb of Raphael."

Zoe spotted Harrington's gray hair and immaculate cream suit.

"Let's go slow," Jack said.

"Right. He doesn't exactly look like he's anxious to see us."

They eased up to Harrington, his gaze focused on a statue of a Madonna and child in the niche above Raphael's tomb.

"Any trouble?" he asked quietly without moving.

"No."

"Good. Take a few moments here then meet me at the first café on the Via della Minerva. I'll be in the back."

2

HARRINGTON MEANDERED AWAY. ZOE AND Jack circled the church, but Zoe couldn't concentrate on the amazing structure anymore. After a few minutes, they slipped back into the noise and sunlight of the piazza where the fountain burbled and the clip-clop of hooves rang out as a horse trotted away, pulling a carriage of sightseers. Zoe consulted the map she'd tucked into her messenger bag and guided them to the side street where they spotted the café.

Inside, the waiter waved them to any table they wanted, and they made their way to the back of the room to join Harrington. From across the room, she thought he looked exactly the same as he had a year ago when he'd presented them with the paperwork for the finder's fee, but now that she was closer, she could see dark circles under his eyes. Zoe supposed he was somewhere in his late fifties. He had a full head of gray hair, a kind face, and a thin mustache that made Zoe think of movie stars from the thirties and forties.

"No, don't kiss me," she said as he took her hand and leaned in to kiss her cheek in the Continental manner. "I'm drenched. I love Rome, but wish it wasn't so blazing hot."

"Unusual for this time of year," Harrington said in his crisp accent as he patted her hand in lieu of the kiss.

"I shouldn't complain," Zoe said as they sat down. "At least it's not raining. That would make site-seeing truly miserable."

The waiter arrived, and Harrington ordered a cup of tea. His posture was casual as he leaned on the table, but he had an edge of alertness in his gaze as he kept an eye on the doorway and studied each new arrival at the café.

"Tea is too hot for me," Zoe said. "I'll have a scoop of lemon gelato." Jack ordered the same.

Harrington ran his hand over his thin mustache and lowered his voice. "Sorry for the intrigue, but it was necessary. As I'm sure you've gathered, this is not a typical job. Tomorrow night at the opening, I will present you with an award, recognition of your role in the return of the art last year. As far as Millbank and Proust are concerned, that is the only reason you are here."

Their order arrived, and Harrington paused until the waiter left. Zoe focused on her tart gelato. Harrington was addressing most of his remarks to Jack. She got it. She was window dressing. Just along for the ride. But she understood. Jack was the expert, and she'd been able to climb the narrow steps of the Colosseum because of this job. Couldn't complain about that.

Harrington stirred his tea as he continued, "There have been several thefts from country homes in England over the last six weeks—all jewelry—all insured by Millbank and Proust."

"And you're concerned about the opening," Jack said.

"Yes. The jewels on display are just too tempting." He loosened his tie a bit and continued as if the words were difficult to get out. "Unfortunately, it appears that the thefts are connected with Millbank and Proust. Certain details that were only known within the company were exploited in the last few instances."

Zoe asked, "Have the thefts been in the news? I don't remember hearing about anything like that lately. Well, except for the heist at the London movie premiere."

Harrington nodded. "Unfortunately, Millbank and Proust was also an insurer for some of those jewels as well. The police have not been able to recover any of the jewels. Except for the theft at the premiere, we have been able to keep the other incidents quiet, so there has been nothing else in the media. He cannot be allowed to strike again."

"He?" Jack asked.

"Metaphorically speaking, of course. I have no idea of the thief's gender."

"But couldn't it be different individuals or even different groups?" Zoe asked.

"Coincidence?" He waved his hand before sipping his tea. "An outside possibility, of course. But I'm afraid there is a small likelihood of it being the correct answer. No, the most likely explanation is, unfortunately for Millbank and Proust, that we have a thief in our employ. I have no definite proof or, of course, I would have already taken it to the authorities. All I have is a theory. That is why I need you. Your attendance will not raise any suspicions. In the past, we have recognized individuals who have contributed to the success of our company, so your attendance and the award will not raise any eyebrows among my colleagues. The pool of possible suspects is quite small—only two. First, there is Carlo Goccetto, director of our European region."

Jack paused, his spoonful of lemon gelato halfway to his mouth. "You suspect a director of your company?"

Harrington looked pained. "Sadly, it gets worse. Our managing director, Melissa Davray, is also on the short list."

Jack stared at him. "You've got to be kidding me."

"No. I wish I were. I started with all possibilities—everyone who had access to the information. It wasn't a large list to begin with. First, I focused on lower ranking employees, but they all have alibis. Carlo and Melissa are the only two people who had the knowledge, the opportunity, and no alibi. As far-fetched as it sounds, that is where I am. I admit, it is hard even for me to picture either one of them actually committing the crimes themselves. I doubt they would do that, so they must have relayed the information to someone else, a partner, who actually carried out the robberies." He ran his finger along his thin mustache again and shook his head. "Nevertheless, you can see why I need you," he said with a sigh. "I will introduce you to them tomorrow. I'll need you to arrive an hour early."

Harrington set his teacup down with a click and removed a stack of photos from his jacket pocket. "This is what I'm most worried about."

The first one, a close-up photo, showed a necklace of diamonds with matching earrings and a bracelet. Even in the dim light and on paper, the gems were amazing. Zoe recognized them. The exhibit traced the history of jewelry from ancient Greek and Roman ornaments up to modern times. This set was one of the relatively modern pieces known as the Flawless Set because each stone was so exquisite. Once owned by a czarina, the set had a fascinating history that included a legendary deathly curse on the owner.

Zoe reached for the stack and glanced through the other photos, which were more close-ups of each piece, front and back, and even a few shots of the hardware, the clasps. She studied the intricate engraving on the clasp on the necklace, an *R* inside an oval.

Harrington noticed her interest. "Jeweler's mark," he

explained. You could see the age of the piece in the clasp. Unlike the diamonds, which looked marvelous, the clasp was a bit beat-up with several scratches, including a long one that ran diagonally across one of the curlicues at the bottom of the *R*, but given that the piece was over one hundred years old, Zoe guessed that wasn't too surprising. Something that old usually had some wear and tear, and she supposed it was another reason diamonds in general were so valuable. Not a speck of deterioration on them, at least that Zoe could see with her untrained eye. She handed the photos back.

Harrington tucked them away. "I personally oversaw the installation earlier this week. I'd like you to stay in the gallery with the Flawless Set all evening tomorrow. It is only two hours and there are quite a few other displays in that room. It is critical I have someone there from the outside."

"You're only worried about tomorrow night?" Jack asked. "If the jewels are there now..."

"Certain factors increase the risk of theft tomorrow night. For the opening, the owner insists on displaying the pieces on a central display with no glass between the exhibit attendees and the jewels. It is one of the draws of opening night. Attendees will be able to see the jewels unimpeded. It is a situation I fought, but the ability to draw a crowd and generate the all-important 'buzz' has trumped my arguments about security. As a fundraiser, one lucky winner will be allowed to wear the Flawless for half an hour."

Jack wiped his hand across his mouth. "So it will be out of the case and transferred from person to person?"

"Out of a case, but not without security. We'll have the usual uniformed and plain-clothed security, video surveillance, and a few other measures that I can't discuss."

"Sounds as if you've got it covered as well as you can."

He looked doubtful. "Yes, well. Needs must and all that," he said with a faint smile. Zoe studied his worried face and wondered how close he was to retirement. If he were paying them out of his own pocket—and he had to be since the job was off the books—he had to be worried about not only the thefts, but his own job.

The bill arrived and both Harrington and Jack reached for their wallets. "No, this one is on me," Harrington said. A folded piece of paper fell out of Harrington's pocket as he removed his wallet. Zoe picked it up and saw the glossy brochure advertised various walking tours.

"Thank you." Harrington took the paper as he left a ten-euro note for their bill. He tapped the brochure. "Excellent tours. I highly recommend the Obelisks of Rome Night Walk. Takes you to all the best bits. Nice overview of the city. Would you like to keep it?"

"Sure. I'm always up for a good night walk," Zoe said, tucking the flyer into her messenger bag.

"Now, tell me what you've seen," Harrington said.

Zoe described their sightseeing as Harrington nodded his approval. "Don't forget to go to the Trevi. Horribly overrun with tourists, but what can you do? You have to throw a coin in," he said, referring to the legend that if you threw a coin in the Trevi Fountain, you'd return to Rome.

Zoe looked at Jack. "Well, we *have* to do that."

"I do it every time I'm here. Insurance," Harrington said with a wink.

"Makes sense," Jack said. "You are an insurance man."

"I wish I could be here more. I find the Roman sun a nice antidote to the rain of London. That's where I'm based, you see."

"Are you able to visit Rome often?" Zoe asked.

"Not as often as I'd like. I hope to retire here. Well, not Rome itself. Too expensive, but a place along the coast would be nice."

He leaned forward as if he had something to confide, but then he seemed to think better of it and checked himself. Instead, he glanced at his watch. "Must get back. I am at the Hotel Santa Maria, but it would be better…"

"I'll only get in touch if it's an emergency," Jack said. "You go first, we'll follow later."

"Want an espresso?" Jack asked after Harrington left.

"In this heat? No way. I'll take a Sprite or ginger ale, if we're burning time."

Jack ordered their drinks. "So not quite the routine job. I should have realized something was up when he offered to pay for our travel to Europe. And he called me, never emailed. His calls always came in the evening, his time. He wasn't calling from the office."

"So? He takes work home, like lots of other people. Nothing unusual there. Has it been long enough? I want to see the Piazza Navona on the way back to the hotel."

"Yeah, I think it's fine." They paid for their drinks and hit the cobblestone streets again. As they strolled down a quiet street away from the Pantheon, Zoe stopped abruptly.

Jack looked up from the map. "What is it?"

"I thought I saw Harrington, up there ahead of us, going into that building." She nodded at a salmon building with brown shutters and green double doors. "But it couldn't have been him. Those are apartments, not a hotel."

"Maybe he's visiting a friend," Jack said, but Zoe saw him take an extra-long look as they walked by.

3

G EMMA NEELEY, OF SCOTLAND YARD'S Art Squad, did not look up from the catalogue of Dutch paintings when she sensed that someone had stopped in front of her desk.

"I'm not going to the pub with you, Davy," she said in her American accent. "I already told you that. Doesn't matter what you call it, that's not football." Gemma had strong feelings about football, having spent her childhood after her parents' divorce shuttling back and forth across the Atlantic between her English mum and her American dad, who was a staunch Green Bay Packers fan. She had other reasons she wasn't going to the pub with Davy, but she kept those to herself. Better to let him think it was the football thing.

"Davy giving you problems, Gemma?"

She looked up and saw the office's fluorescent lights shining on the dome of Nigel Edwards, her boss and the head of the Art Squad. He'd taken the razor to his patchy hair growth last year, declaring that he'd rather resign than resort to a comb-over at the ripe old age of thirty-four.

"Nothing I can't handle," Gemma said. At six-foot-two with

golden blond hair, blue eyes, and a curvy figure that couldn't be disguised, even swathed in a trench coat against London's fickle weather, Gemma stood out in the mostly masculine police world. She had plenty of experience deflecting and diffusing passes. She rolled her chair back a few inches. "What's up?" As much as she liked her easy-going boss, she knew he hadn't dropped by her desk to chat.

"Got word that there's an informant who says he has information on the country house robberies."

Gemma frowned at the art catalogue on her desk. She was working on a cold case, a painting that had been stolen ten years earlier during a break-in at a pitifully ill-secured regional museum. The painting was beautiful—an exquisitely detailed still life of a table, post meal. Messy and realistic, it showed a ruched tablecloth littered with breadcrumbs, tilted glasses, and a half-peeled lemon, its rind curling over the edge of the table. The artist was Willem Claesz. Not exactly a household name. Not like Vermeer or Rembrandt.

Nigel lifted his chin toward the catalogue. "Anything on the Claesz?"

"No," Gemma said, reluctantly. "Just going over everything, looking for something that was missed the first time."

Nigel nodded, his dark brown gaze on the catalogue, too. "If we get a break on the country house thefts, it would be good for the department. Higher ups are rumbling about cutting our budget."

"Again?"

"Some idiot has floated the idea of closing the department altogether. That way, they could shift all our funding to terrorism."

"Well, can't blame them. Lot easier to justify funds to prevent terrorists from killing citizens than to find a dusty old painting," she said with a downward quirk of her lips. The budget battle was a constant threat. The Art Squad was the easiest thing to cut.

Her boss waited a beat. "But jewels make headlines."

"Unlike poor Claesz." If they recovered the Claesz, it might get a mention or two, buried at the bottom of the day's news. If they found a stash of missing jewels, it would be headline news.

Gemma slapped a sticky note on the corner of the page then closed the catalogue. She took the paper Nigel held out. "Well, let's see if we can find something and get a nice splashy headline to keep the bean counters at bay."

"That's not the way the zipper goes." Zoe looked over her shoulder at Jack.

"I thought you wanted my help with it."

"Zipping it up, not down."

He reversed course with the zipper. "Pity," he said as he fastened the tiny hook at the top of the zipper, his breath fanning over her bare shoulders, making her shiver. "Don't tempt me." Zoe shot him a look as she crossed the room, her dress swishing around her, and stepped into her shoes, stilettos that she'd borrowed from her friend Helen's well-stocked closet. "You look tempting in that tux, but you're the one who promised Harrington we'd be there an hour early."

"I knew we shouldn't have tried to work in the Castel Sant'Angelo." He adjusted his cuffs and held out his arm.

Zoe gave herself one final check in the mirror and rubbed her collarbone. "I shouldn't have gotten so much sun today. My freckles are really popping." She reached for her makeup bag.

Jack crossed the room and caught her hand. "Your freckles are incredibly sexy."

She laughed. "No they're not. Spotty, blotchy patches are not sexy."

He pulled her into his arms. "Yes they are."

"Then why don't you see lots of models or actresses with freckles?"

"Hollywood and the media are messed up."

"Well, that is true. I'll give you that point, but think about it. All those statues and paintings we've been looking at, how many freckles did you see? None. Freckles aren't attractive."

"Yes, they are." Jack studied her face then said, "I can see I need to demonstrate. Perhaps kiss each one?"

"Then we'll be so late, the opening will be over."

"Later, then?" Jack raised an eyebrow.

"Definitely."

Gray clouds slid across the sky as they emerged from the hotel, and Zoe hoped it wasn't about to rain. If it did, the increased humidity would erase the smooth lines she'd flat-ironed into her hair and tease out her natural curls, giving her more of a Little Orphan Annie look. At least her hair was up. She'd spent half an hour twisting her hair into a soft chignon, using several strategically placed hairpins decorated with tiny navy blue beads. If the humidity did descend, at least the frizz wouldn't be quite so noticeable.

They took a taxi to the museum, which was located a few blocks off the Piazza del Popolo in the northwest of the city. The first raindrops spattered down as they hurried up the steps to the palazzo that had been converted to a museum. They gave their invitation to a young woman at the door with flyaway brown hair and an elfin face who was juggling a phone and a clipboard while she kept reaching up to adjust an earpiece that continually slipped out of her ear. "Oh, Mr. Throckmorton is waiting for you. This way, please." She guided them through the grand entrance hall to a gallery that ran around a central courtyard. Weathered statues, most of them missing limbs, and often their heads as well, lined the interior wall.

"See—zero freckles," Zoe said softly.

Jack raised an eyebrow languidly. "Their loss."

Their escort said, "This is the end of the exhibit, the last room, but Mr. Throckmorton said to bring you directly here." They entered the spacious room with mosaics on the floor and a heavy wood-beamed ceiling. Partial frescoes of rural scenes decorated the walls and more statues ranged around the edges of the room, but it was the jewels displayed in the center of the room that had everyone's attention.

Zoe could see why they would save these pieces for last. The gems glittered and sparkled. The contrast of their modern crafts-manship—relatively speaking—against the ancient art of the stat-ues, frescoes, and mosaics only emphasized their sophisticated beauty.

Harrington saw them and moved across the room. He was also looking distinguished in a tuxedo. "Thank you, Amy," he said to the young woman and she left, hastily grabbing her earpiece as it slipped again.

"My new assistant." He winced as Amy narrowly avoided a collision with a waiter holding a tray of appetizers. He turned to them and shook hands with Jack. "Good to see you. And you look lovely." He kissed Zoe's cheek, and she almost made a quip about not being too sweaty for a kiss, but stopped herself. They weren't supposed to have met for a year. She thanked him instead.

A handsome man in his thirties with black hair threaded with silver at the temples, black eyes, and a roguish smile joined their group, his gaze fixed on Zoe. "Harrington, is this the lovely crea-ture who rescued your piece that had gone missing?"

"Yes, we are indebted to Mrs. Andrews. Carlo Goccetto, head of Millbank and Proust's European region," Harrington said as he introduced them, and Zoe didn't miss the significant glance that passed between Jack and Harrington while Carlo kissed the back of her hand.

Zoe disengaged her hand from his slightly damp palm. "And this is my husband, Jack."

Carlo flicked a glance at Jack. "Delighted."

"Both Mr. and Mrs. Andrews played a vital role in the return," Harrington said, giving the titles a slight emphasis, which Carlo either completely missed or ignored.

"Have you seen the exhibit, yet?" Carlo asked Zoe.

"No. We just arrived."

"May I?"

Zoe opened her mouth to refuse, but Jack cut her off. "Go ahead, I'll catch up. I need to make a phone call."

Zoe sent Jack a dark glance as Carlo extended his elbow. Jack leaned in and whispered, "I know you can handle him. Find out what you can."

As Carlo pulled her away, she looked over her shoulder and mouthed, "You owe me." They moved through the chain of rooms to the beginning of the exhibit, then they retraced their steps, looking at coiled gold Minoan earrings, Greek cameos, bracelets from Pompeii, and rough gold crosses. Zoe admired the pieces, and Carlo told her interesting stories about some of the jewelry.

"Did you know Caesar was obsessed with pearls?" he asked as they looked at a large pink-tinted pearl.

"No," Zoe said, using the excuse of leaning closer to the case to wiggle her hand free of his arm, but he adjusted his stance, moved with her, and kept her hand firmly tucked into the crook of his elbow.

"He even had a law passed to prevent anyone from owning pearls except the aristocracy."

Zoe murmured an appropriate reply, and he towed her along

to the next room. "They're all so beautiful," Zoe said as they moved by the heavy medieval pieces to more delicate Renaissance jewelry studded with gems. "Can you imagine having one of these?"

His mouth curved down into a frown. "Too much trouble," he said quietly. "Believe me, I know. The insurance, the security. No, I enjoy them, but I would not want to own any of these jewels."

"Even the Flawless Set?" Zoe asked, hoping she wasn't being too obvious.

"Ah, that would be the worst of all," he said. "The notoriety alone..." he trailed off, squeezing her hand tighter to his side. "No, I prefer other things of beauty."

Zoe was glad to see they were almost back to the last room where Jack was moving through the crowd toward them. As they entered the final room again, Harrington's assistant, Amy, careened through the doorway and ran directly into Zoe, knocking her back against the doorframe.

"Oh! I am so sorry."

"It's okay." Zoe felt her upswept hair slip to the nape of her neck and looked down to see several of the beaded hairpins on the mosaic floor.

"I'm so, so sorry." Amy flushed and scrambled on the floor for the pins, turning an even deeper crimson when she saw Carlo glowering at her as he knelt down to help her.

"Nothing that can't be fixed." Zoe took the pins from Amy's shaking hand and Carlo's slightly damp palm, thinking that it was too bad she couldn't thank the girl for giving her the perfect excuse to ditch Carlo. Zoe stopped Amy in mid-apology, told her with a significant look at Carlo that it was nothing to worry about, and left for the restroom.

"Learn anything?" Jack asked when she joined him later. He removed disks of deep-fried bread topped with dollops of buffalo mozzarella and a basil leaf off a tray and handed one to her.

"Only that he has excellent triceps."

Jack did a double take.

"He kept my arm pinned to his side the whole time."

"I see."

They spent the rest of the evening in the final gallery surrounded by the exquisite jewelry, and even though it was almost two hours, Zoe wasn't bored. She admired the jewelry, especially the Flawless Set. The diamonds flashed and glittered under the lights. The necklace was the most spectacular of the three pieces, a string of graduated round-cut diamonds that began small, about the size of a pea, at the clasp and gradually increased in size to the largest stones in the front, which were bigger than Zoe's thumbnail. Zoe walked slowly around the necklace, amazed at how large even the small stones were. Then she looked at the matching bracelet, a single string of diamonds, as well as the earrings, which were two medium round-cut earrings in simple settings. It was the most popular piece and people invariably entered the room and moved directly to it.

"What do you think?" purred a voice behind her shoulder. "Beautiful, no?"

Zoe shifted so that Carlo was not directly behind her. He was slightly shorter than Zoe was, and his hot breath doused her shoulder. Unlike the pleasant shivers Jack's breath on her bare skin had given her earlier, this guy's panting made her long for a cocktail napkin.

"Yes, they are gorgeous," she agreed. She looked back, expecting to find him staring at her as he had during their tour of the exhibit, but now he fixed his gaze on the Flawless Set. So much for not wanting it, Zoe thought. The guy was all but drooling.

"A few people do not like it," he said. "They say the design, the setting, is too simple, that it is crude, even boring. What do you think?"

"I think the stones are so beautiful that they don't need elaborate settings or extra gems to enhance them."

He dragged his gaze away from the stones to her face. "Exactly. Yes, that is it. You put it so well. There is a painting—very fine—in the gallery upstairs. Perhaps I could show you..."

"Oh, my husband wants me. Excuse me," she said, extracting her hand from his sweaty grip.

Jack was busy, keeping an eye on things while seeming to be doing nothing else except to stroll around the room. He was good at that—appearing completely relaxed on the surface, but being on high alert underneath. She joined him. As they admired a statue twisted into what looked to be a truly painful position, Jack said, "What do you think of him?"

"Carlo?"

Jack raised an eyebrow.

"Well, what else am I supposed to call him? Mr. Goccetto?"

"It would make me feel better, yes. He seems quite the ladies' man."

"He's got sweaty palms and is more interested in the diamonds than any woman in the room."

Jack looked happier as they went to look at a floor mosaic. Zoe had been fascinated with mosaics ever since she toured Pompeii, and there were some fine examples fitted into the floor of the room. Zoe studied the scene of gladiators fighting while Jack appeared to be doing the same, but he was keeping an eye on the people moving through the room.

A thin blond woman in her mid-forties with an air of energy barely under control announced it was time for the conclusion of the "Be Flawless" fundraising campaign. She made the announcement in a crisp upper crust English accent then repeated it in

Italian and German. At least that's what it sounded like to Zoe. The blond woman drew a name from a crystal bowl, and a well-preserved brunette was allowed to wear the Flawless Set, minus the bracelet because the clasp broke as Harrington tried to put it on the lucky lady. But the winner didn't seem to mind too much. She kept running her hand over the necklace and fingering the earrings.

She had her photo taken and mingled with uniformed security officers following a pace behind her. Jack watched everything with a lazy posture and sharp eyes. Zoe was sure there were more security guards in tuxedos as well. After the winner circled the room and multiple photos were taken, Harrington removed the necklace and earrings and placed them on their black velvet display beside the bracelet.

All eyes were on the jewels as the transfer was made until the clatter of shattering glass jerked everyone's attention to the back of the room where a flushed waiter was already scrambling to clean up his dropped tray.

Zoe looked back toward Harrington and saw that the jewels were in place and the glass case was being lowered over them. One of the worker's hands slipped, and he bumped the case, knocking the jewels out of their velvet indentations. Harrington quickly replaced them. "No harm done," he said. "Slowly, this time."

The glass was positioned and secured with screws as another man with a laptop approached. Zoe assumed he was checking those mysterious "other security protocols" that Harrington hadn't been able to discuss with them. Jack had told her that displays often had sensors or pressure plates installed to prevent theft.

The energetic trilingual woman swept in front of the jewels with a rustle of silk, the folds of her one-shoulder black mermaid gown flickering around her feet. She made her announcement, again in three languages. "As a finale this evening, we are pleased to present the Millbank and Proust Award to two people who provided a great service to the arts. It was through their actions that a priceless masterpiece was preserved and returned to its rightful owner. " Amy, her earpiece still slipping, appeared at the woman's elbow with a wooden plaque. Without glancing at her, the woman took it and swept an arm toward Jack and Zoe as she announced their names.

They made their way through the crowd, and a smattering of applause briefly filled the room. Jack murmured, "Harrington didn't say we'd have to speak."

"We'll wing it."

They accepted the award, shook hands, deposited air kisses, and then everyone looked to Jack for a few words. He looked back, a smile on his face, but Zoe saw the tension in his hands as he gripped the plaque, his knuckles going white. He glanced at her, and she said thank you in three languages. "And that is all we can say. That is the extent of my German," she said with a shrug.

The audience laughed and the blond woman thanked everyone for coming. Jack handed Zoe the plaque. It was about an inch and a half thick and had a shiny metal plate affixed to the front with an engraving that proclaimed they had provided valuable assistance to Millbank and Proust, as well as the artistic community. "Well done. My mind went completely blank. They liked you."

"Oh, they were just glad they didn't have to listen to a speech," Zoe said as the woman in the mermaid dress moved to their elbow.

She said, "So sorry we did not meet earlier. I am Melissa Davray."

Harrington appeared as well. "Melissa is our managing director," Harrington said as if he hadn't briefed them on Melissa earlier. Zoe tried not to gawk. Could this impeccably groomed and obviously successful woman possibly be a jewel thief? Diamond accented combs held her elaborate updo in place so she must not be short of funds herself. Why would she risk everything? Zoe's gaze strayed to the Flawless Set. It was beautifully spectacular. Of course, she couldn't picture the damp-palmed Carlo carrying out a robbery either.

Jack was no longer tongue-tied and smoothly thanked her for the award and the opportunity to attend the opening.

"You are most welcome." Melissa turned to Zoe, the translucent skin at the corners of her almond shaped eyes wrinkling as she smiled. "It is an event that appeals more to women than to men, I think. All women love bling, as you say in the States, I believe."

"I certainly enjoyed the bling," Zoe said.

"Oh, there is someone I must speak with," she said and was off before anyone could say anything else.

Harrington watched her go. "I do wonder sometimes if she actually sleeps. She's always on the move. Doesn't even use her office chair." Now that the cover was secured over the jewels, he looked more relaxed.

He extended a hand to Jack with a barely noticeable tilt of his head to the Flawless Set. "Thank you for everything. Perhaps we could meet for lunch tomorrow?"

They agreed on a restaurant, and Zoe and Jack joined the crowd exiting the building. Thunder rumbled and rain spattered them as they climbed into another taxi. "Well, that was anticlimactic," Zoe said. "No smash and grab, no theft, no excitement at all."

"Anticlimactic is good," Jack said. "Especially in the security business." He ran his arm along the backseat of the taxi and turned to her. "Now we have a pressing matter to discuss. Freckles."

"Odd that Harrington didn't show up," Zoe said as they climbed the stairs to their hotel room the next day. They'd spent the morning meandering through the streets with no agenda or tourist site on their program, except for lunch with Harrington. They'd waited an hour at the pizzeria that he and Jack had agreed on, again, a few blocks from the Pantheon, but he hadn't arrived. After trying several appetizers while they waited, they'd finally decided he must have been delayed and split a pizza dotted with milky buffalo mozzarella and disks of Roma tomatoes.

"Yes, he's usually so reliable." Jack pulled his phone from his pocket.

Zoe unlocked their door. "Still nothing?"

"No. I'll try him again. He always calls back."

Zoe tossed the key on the dresser and set down their single souvenir purchase, a line drawing of the Spanish Steps, which they'd climbed earlier that day. They had begun at the crush around the unpretentious, almost whimsical, boat-like fountain at the base, stopped at the pink house on the right, where Keats lived and died, then scaled the wide marble steps that split and wrapped around to a high terrace with another obelisk. Harrington's brochure informed them the obelisk was a Roman replica with some funky errors in the hieroglyphs that had been copied from the obelisk in the nearby Piazza del Popolo.

Zoe pulled out a change of clothes and headed for the bathroom. "I'm taking a shower." The morning tour of Rome had been wonderful, but she was sticky and hot. Jack nodded as he dialed.

She luxuriated in the cool spray. They had air conditioning in their room, but it wasn't like the frigid central air she was used to in Texas. As she stepped out of the shower, she heard voices in their room, a tenor to the counterpoint of Jack's baritone.

She caught a few words. Harrington's name was mentioned along with what sounded like the words "jewelry" and "fake."

With her towel still wrapped around her, she leaned her ear against the door.

The tenor voice was saying, "...Throckmorton's assistant was completing her routine check of each display at the exhibit this morning when she discovered the substitution. From the time the Flawless Set arrived here in Rome—when it was authenticated by an independent expert to be the true and rare set of jewels—until this morning, the only person who had full access to the pieces was Signor Throckmorton. He is missing."

Jack's voice cut in sharply, "Missing?"

"Yes. His hotel room is empty. He is not answering his mobile, and no one has seen him since last night. Where is he?"

"I have no idea. We were supposed to meet for lunch, but he didn't show up."

"Was that part of the plan?"

"What plan?"

"Your plan with Signor Throckmorton to steal the Flawless Set."

"I don't know what you are talking about." Jack's voice had gone to a quiet level that set off alarm bells for Zoe. He only spoke that way when he was angry or upset.

The other man continued as if Jack had not spoken. "You see, the bracelet in the display case has a complete clasp. It is not broken. The display case has not been opened since last night— we know this because it has a computer sensor attached to it that records all movement, very high tech, is how it is phrased, no? Therefore, a substitution has been made. The real diamond bracelet has been replaced with a fake, as have all the other gems. The necklace, bracelet, and earrings on display this morning are copies. Since the case has not been opened since Signor Throckmorton placed the jewels inside it last night, we must conclude that he made the switch last night during the exhibit opening."

"And how could he make the switch with everyone watching him?"

"Sleight of hand. Even a passable magician can distract. The waiter tripped and dropped his tray. The crash drew everyone's attention away from the diamonds. Signor Throckmorton palmed the real set and replaced it with the fakes, which he must have had hidden in his sleeves."

"But you're talking about three separate pieces of jewelry—no four, if you count the earrings individually. He couldn't change out that many separate pieces in a few seconds without someone knowing."

"Ah, but there was another disturbance. Remember the 'accident' when the worker bumped the display? Perhaps it was no accident? Two interruptions would be plenty of time for him to make the change. None of it—even the earrings were to be displayed hanging. All of it was to rest on the velvet cushions, which would make fast transfers possible. Signor Throckmorton personally arranged for the gems to be displayed in this fashion."

Zoe pushed away from the door and hurriedly slipped into her clothes, a pair of white shorts and a lightweight turquoise top. Those accusations were absurd. The idea that someone could switch several pieces of jewelry without anyone noticing was ridiculous. The volume of the voices escalated as she grabbed her towel off the counter to toss it over the towel rack. It caught on her quilted jewelry bag, pulling it off the counter. It hit the tile floor, and her jewelry scattered around her feet.

As she crouched down to gather up hoop earrings and thin gold chains, she froze, staring at a diamond bracelet that had tumbled from the bag and lay in a sinuous "S" curve on the towel bathmat in front of the shower. The glittering, icy-clear stones sparkled, looking as out of place and foreign as a snake, but still as beautiful and striking as it had last night when she'd looked at it during the exhibit. It was the bracelet from the Flawless Set.

The tenor voice went up another notch, and Zoe could clearly hear the man say, "Then you won't object if we have a look around?"

Zoe scuttled closer to the seam of the door. "Of course not," Jack said. "But it is ridiculous to even consider that Harrington or Zoe and I could be involved in any way."

"And your wife is where?"

"In the bath. She'll be out in a moment."

A knock on the door caused it to vibrate, and Zoe jumped back, stifling a gasp.

"Zoe," Jack said. "We have company. Colonel Alessi from the Carabinieri. There's been some sort of mix-up."

Zoe looked back at the bracelet and licked her lips. "Be right out." She scrambled around the floor, stuffing her jewelry in the quilted travel bag until the floor was clear except for the diamond bracelet.

She crawled closer. It couldn't be the bracelet from the Flawless Set. It just couldn't. Maybe somehow, someway, an imitation bracelet had gotten in her jewelry bag. She didn't know how that could happen, but the thought of the bracelet just appearing out of nowhere and now the police were here, talking about missing jewelry...it was just too odd.

She crouched lower and looked at the bracelet, her nose only inches from the bathmat, and her heart sank. The jewels themselves were dazzling, but it was the clasp that she was fixated on. It was scored and worn and had the 'R' inside an oval, just like the clasp on the necklace, and the clasp was broken—just like the piece from the exhibit last night.

Zoe thudded back on her heels. What was she going to do?

On the other side of the door, she could hear drawers opening and closing. It wouldn't be long before they'd insist she come out of the bathroom and let them search. Should she take it out there with her, and say she'd just found it?

Would the Carabinieri believe her? What if they didn't? Zoe bit her lip. Worst-case scenario, Jack and she would be carted off to a police station and wrapped up in red tape and probably a jail cell for...well, she didn't know how long. That didn't sound like a good plan, but what else could she do? Hide it? From the sounds on the other side of the door, the search was thorough. And then what? Return it—somehow—anonymously?

They definitely needed time to figure out what do to. Maybe they could go to the American Embassy and have the bracelet returned through official channels. Yes, that sounded much better. At least that way they wouldn't start out in a jail cell.

Her gaze darted around, looking for a hiding place, but the bathroom didn't have cabinets or drawers, just a freestanding counter with a sink, a shower, a towel rack, a toilet, and a bidet. She scrambled to look under the counter, but there were no gaps or ridges where she could place the bracelet. The toilet tank was an old stand-by hiding place that she'd seen used in movies. Surely that was too common and it would be searched. What was left? The shower drain and an air vent were both screwed into place and she wouldn't be able to get them loose without considerable time and lots of work with a nail file, so those were out.

"Zoe, you okay?" Jack asked.

"Yes, fine. I'll be out in a minute."

Her shorts had pockets, but their clothes might be searched as well. She might not have a choice. She might have to turn it over right now. She felt herself breaking out in a cold sweat. She'd been in the position of being under suspicion before, and it wasn't something she wanted to repeat.

She scanned the ceiling, saw the light fixture, and was up on the toilet lid before she'd had time to think it through. She couldn't reach it. She hopped back down, frantically scanning the room. There had to be something—her gaze landed on the travel-size bottle of lotion.

The bracelet was still on the bathmat. She hesitated a second before picking it up. Touching it seemed like a commitment, a commitment to a path that put them in opposition to the police.

"Mrs. Andrews," the tenor voice said, "we request you join us."

"Yes. Of course. Sorry." She quickly unscrewed the cap on the opaque bottle of lotion then used a tissue to pick up the bracelet. She didn't want even the faintest trace of a fingerprint on the bracelet. It was much heavier than she'd expected. She transferred it to the lotion bottle and was relieved when all the stones slipped easily through the opening. A little lotion oozed over the side as the last diamond went in. Zoe wiped it off, capped the bottle, gave it a few shakes to make sure it was at the bottom and covered by lotion, and then tossed the tissue in the trash. The bottle felt a little heavy, but she couldn't do anything about that. She tightened her grip around it for a second, wanting to put it in her pocket, but that would draw attention to it, especially if the police searched her pockets. No, better to leave it in plain sight. She shoved it into the line along the back of the counter with her makeup.

She massaged the rest of the lotion into her hands then opened the door, and a man nearly fell into the bathroom. He was about Zoe's height, had a slight build, and his thick eyebrows were drawn together in a scowl that created wrinkles at the bridge of his nose. "Ah, Signora Andrews. Good of you to join us. I am Colonel Alessi."

He didn't extend his hand for Zoe to shake it, so she nodded and moved across the room to join Jack where he stood near the balcony. For someone who didn't know him, his casual posture of crossed arms as he leaned against the balcony door might have looked relaxed, but Zoe could tell from the glowering look in his eyes that he was furious. "Did you hear what was said?" Jack asked, his voice tight.

"Enough."

A second, younger man accompanied Alessi. He stood up from where he'd been peering under the bed and dusted off his pants. Alessi jerked his head toward the bath, and the young man disappeared through the door.

"It's best to let them have their look around," Jack said. "Then they'll see we have nothing to hide."

"Yes, I suppose so," Zoe said and sent him a warning glance.

Jack's didn't move, but his gaze sharpened on her. He pushed away from the wall. "Since you've already searched the balcony, you don't have any objection to my wife sitting there, do you?" The sentence wasn't phrased as a question, and Jack was already moving so that Zoe could step outside before Alessi gave a disinterested wave of the hand. He was focused on the award plaque that he'd picked up from the dresser.

"Do we have something to hide?" he asked in a low voice as she moved by him.

"Yes," she breathed. She took a seat and sent a quick, pointed gaze to the bathroom. The shower door clicked as the officer open it, glanced inside, and then closed it. He moved out of their line of sight, and Zoe heard the ceramic toilet tank lid clink as he moved it. Good thing she hadn't put it in there. More clinking as he replaced the lid. The young officer came into view again, his back to them, as he scanned the counter around the sink. Zoe forced herself to look away, even though she wanted to stare at the lotion bottle.

She looked at Alessi, who was turning the plaque slowly in his hand, examining each surface. He moved a few steps closer to them and angled it toward the light streaming in through the windows as he ran his thumbnail along the thick edge of the plaque. He glanced at them once, a long measuring glance, then removed a Swiss Army knife from his pocket, extended one of the blades, and inserted it into what looked like a dark thread in the grain of the wood.

The knife blade twisted, flashing in the sun, and the thin dark line widened into a gap. Alessi worked the knife blade back and forth a few more times, and the gap broadened until he was able to put his thumbs on the edges and pry. The plaque split into two pieces, exposing a foam center with cutouts for a necklace, a bracelet, and two earrings.

4

GEMMA PULLED INTO A SLOT along the curb across the street from Croftly Jewelers. A dark blue awning shaded the shop's single front window, which held a display of diamond necklaces and earrings. When she'd met with the informant, he had pushed his long hair back off his face and said, "All I know is me mate said that the guy's name is Terrance Croftly, and that he's got a medieval cross that he's pulling stones out of."

A ninth-century jewel-encrusted cross had been stolen from Gilbrand House. Of course the informant hadn't seen the cross himself and couldn't describe it.

"And why would this Terrance Croftly flash around something as distinctive as a medieval cross?" Gemma had asked.

"He weren't," the informant had said. "Me mate, the one who told me about it, saw it by accident. He works the counter, doesn't usually go in the back. Surprised 'em, I guess."

Gemma doubted that was exactly the way it had happened, but regardless, they had the tip.

The shop looked like the other small-to-medium businesses in London's diamond district. Gemma tapped the wheel, wishing she could go in as a customer for a quick browse, but that would be a mistake, if she had to go in later undercover.

She was good undercover. It was how she first connected with the Art Squad. They needed someone who didn't look or sound like a cop and had pulled her from traffic duty to play the part of a dodgy American dealer anxious to buy a stolen painting. When she met the thieves, her accent and her gender, two things that had often been negatives in her career, worked as assets and had put the criminals at ease. The bust had gone like clockwork. Within a year, she was able to transfer to the Art Squad.

Gemma returned to the office and pulled everything she could find on Terrance Croftly.

Zoe leaned over the table, her gaze locked on Alessi's face. "I don't know anything about the plaque, except that Melissa Davray gave it to us at the opening of the exhibit." The plaque, now encased in a transparent plastic bag, rested on the table between her and Alessi. They were in some sort of police station. Zoe wasn't even sure if it was a police station or an office of the Carabinieri.

After Alessi discovered the interior compartment in the plaque, he'd called the younger officer out of the bathroom, which had been a relief for Zoe, but then Alessi had insisted Jack and Zoe come with him and give an official statement. Jack had objected, but Alessi had been firm. They could either come willingly or in handcuffs. Since they didn't have a choice, they'd gone with him, but Jack had used the cell phone to find a phone number for the American Embassy and had called it while they were on the way. Alessi hadn't liked that. His frown deepened, but he hadn't stopped Jack either. Unfortunately, when Jack explained their situation, the American official took down the details and said he would get back to them soon.

They'd been separated, and Zoe had waited at least an hour in the stuffy room before Alessi threw open the door and placed the plastic bag on the table.

Zoe rubbed her forehead. "Look, my answers aren't changing. Your questions aren't changing. We've been over this—many times. We took the plaque back to our hotel room and put it on the dresser. We didn't examine it or try to pry it open like you did. We just set it down and went on with our sightseeing. Instead of being so interested in Harrington, I'm surprised you're not asking about Melissa Davray. She was the one who gave it to us." She considered telling him about Harrington's theory of a thief in the company, but Alessi's questions hadn't gone there yet, and the last thing she wanted to do was give him a new avenue to explore. So far, he was mostly interested in the plaque. And, Harrington himself had admitted that he had no proof of a thief within Millbank and Proust, only a theory.

She was sure Jack would stick as closely to the truth as possible, but given his recent run-ins with police when he'd been wrongly accused, Zoe was sure he wouldn't give up the details about Harrington and the real reason for their trip to Rome. If she volunteered the info when Jack hadn't, it wouldn't look good for her or Jack. And considering she had stuffed several million dollars' worth of diamonds into a lotion bottle back at the hotel, she wanted to keep this encounter as short as possible. The less said, the better.

Alessi said, "Every possibility will be considered, but at this point, you and your husband are a special case. This morning, we received information that you, your husband, and Harrington Throckmorton stole the diamonds. Signor Throckmorton cannot be found, and you and your husband had in your possession a plaque, which you obviously used to remove the diamonds from the exhibit last night, so I'm sure you can understand why we are so interested in you. Tell me, Signora Andrews, was it Signor Throckmorton's idea? Did he come to you and your husband? Or have you perhaps done this before?"

Zoe closed her eyes for a second and fought off the sheer panic that rose inside her. "I've told you—there wasn't any plan to steal anything. Harrington contacted Jack about the award. We didn't know anything about the plaque being hollow. As I said, we didn't see it or know about it until Mrs. Davray handed it to us. Harrington only said it was an award. I thought it would be a certificate or something like that."

"Ah, but Signora Davray says it was Signor Throckmorton who coordinated everything involved with the plaque. How often were you in contact with him?"

"Me? Never. He contacted Jack."

"And how many times did you meet with him to plan this robbery?"

Zoe muttered, "It's like talking to a brick wall." In her normal voice, she said, "We never met to talk about a robbery."

Alessi jumped on her words. "But you said earlier that you met yesterday."

"Yes, we met, but—as I also said earlier—we discussed the award."

The scowl that seemed to be permanently etched between Alessi's eyebrows deepened. "It was his suggestion for the company to give you the award and pay for your travel here to Rome. He arranged it all."

"But that doesn't mean he planned to replace the Flawless Set with fakes and smuggle the real ones out in the plaque." Zoe tapped the plastic bag. "This could be a distraction."

Alessi's frown eased as he leaned back in his chair. "A red

herring, you mean? As in a crime novel? No, I am afraid that thieves are rarely as clever in real life as they are in fiction."

After two more rounds of the same questions, Alessi left and a paper with her statement was produced. She signed it and was escorted into a long hallway where a woman barreled out of one of the doors and plowed into Zoe. The woman looked familiar and amid the apologies, Zoe took a closer look and realized it was Melissa Davray. Without her hair coiffed around the diamond-studded combs, it fell flat and straight around her face, which looked plain without the dramatic makeup highlighting her eyes and lips. Her boxy gray suit and plain white shirt were about as far as you could get from the mermaid gown, stylistically speaking.

She apologized in Italian, then recognized Zoe. Her expression froze, and she broke off mid-sentence. Switching to English, she said, "So clever, turning one of our own against us. But I will not forget this. You have taken advantage of our gratitude and embarrassed us."

"Wait a minute. We had nothing to do with—"

She stepped forward, forcing Zoe back against the wall. She was so close that Zoe could see the yellow flecks in her hazel eyes. "Alessi may not be able to prove what you did—yet."

Zoe's escort, a compact woman with her hair clipped back in a no-nonsense bun, stepped forward to intervene, but Melissa held out her hand and snapped a few words in Italian that made the woman pause.

Melissa turned back to Zoe, "Your business is built on the 'help' you gave us. I promise you that I will personally see to it that Safe Haven is completely dismantled. You will never have another client after I'm done."

She turned and marched away, her sensible low-heeled pumps clacking on the tile floor.

***

Jack was waiting outside at the foot of the marble steps. Zoe's police escort watched from the top of the steps as Zoe descended. Jack reached out, and Zoe threaded her fingers through his as they strode away from the building at a quick pace.

Jack leaned close. "Did you mention Harrington's suspicion about the thefts?"

"No. You?"

"No."

"Good. I knew you wouldn't."

He shot her a glance, his eyebrows raised as they navigated around tourists consulting a map.

"Don't look surprised. I may not have you totally figured out, but I do know a few things about you. You're quite skittish where the police are concerned."

"With good reason."

"Yes, I'll give you that. So I knew you'd give the least complicated version of the truth and get out of there as soon as possible. I just hope Alessi didn't send someone back to search our room again."

"Why?"

"Because the bracelet from the Flawless Set was in my jewelry bag in the bathroom."

Jack stumbled. "What?"

Zoe recounted how she'd found the bracelet and where she'd hidden it.

"You're sure it was from the Flawless Set?"

"The clasp is broken, just like the one at the exhibit last night, and it had the mark, the *R* in the oval."

"That sounds like the real deal."

"I know. Did Alessi tell you that they got a tip this morning that you and I and Harrington stole the Flawless Set?"

"No, he didn't. No wonder he's leaning so hard on us."

"It can't be true," Zoe said. It was impossible to imagine proper and buttoned-down Harrington stealing.

"No, of course not," Jack said. "But I'm even more worried about him now."

"I know," Zoe said. "I can only think of a few reasons he'd go missing."

"Yes, and none of them are good."

"Maybe he's hurt or sick. Or he could have been in an accident." Zoe rubbed her hand across her forehead. "Listen to me. You know the situation is horrible when the thought of someone being hurt or sick is a positive."

"We'll find him," Jack said confidently. "First, we have to get back to the hotel and take care of that thing you mentioned."

"Where are we?" Zoe looked around for familiar streets or landmarks. They'd been moving along quickly and talking so intently that she hadn't paid attention to where they were.

"We're not far from the hotel, and we have a tail." They stopped to cross a street, and Jack said, "Behind my right shoulder, about fifteen feet back. Receding hairline and a mustache. Gray shirt, black pants. See him?"

Zoe pretended to adjust the strap of her messenger bag as she glanced over Jack's shoulder. She swallowed. "Yes. How long has he been following us?"

"He dropped onto us a block from the police station." The light changed, and they joined a group crossing the street in front of a line of Smart cars and motor scooters. "I'm not sure about the woman with the blue backpack and sunglasses," Jack said as they neared the other side of the street. "She could be following us, too. Looks like Alessi cut us free so he could keep an eye on us, see what we do."

Zoe looked back in time to catch a glimpse of a woman much closer to them with dark hair caught up in a bun.

"I think she may have escorted me out of the police station."

"Thought so," Jack said.

"Should we try to lose them?"

"No, that would look odd."

"Okay, then. Let's go back to our hotel—that's a perfectly normal thing to do, except for the checking on the priceless jewelry part."

"Right. We'll just keep that last thing to ourselves."

They consulted their map and caught a bus that dropped them a few blocks from their hotel. They made their way through the bustling Campo de' Fiori, passing the statue of the hooded philosopher—Zoe couldn't remember his name—but she knew the somber figure had been burned in the campo for heresy during the Inquisition. The statue had always seemed such a sharp contrast to the busy market of vendors selling fruit and vegetables, spices, flowers, and specialty foods as well as the crowds gathering at open-air restaurants that ringed the square. The statue looked especially forbidding today.

Zoe tried to shake off the bleak feeling as they moved into the street off the campo and paused at the hotel's front desk. The desk clerk was away, so Jack stepped around the counter and removed their key from its pigeonhole in the wall.

They climbed the steps to their room, and Zoe went directly to the bath. The little bottle was still there, and it still felt slightly heavier than a normal bottle of lotion. She turned toward Jack to tell him, but he was near the window, positioned with his back to the wall so that it would be difficult for someone outside to see him.

Zoe crossed the room. "Are they there?"

"Yes, one of them, anyway. Mustache Guy is waiting at the corner."

She raised the bottle. "Still here."

"Did you check?" Jack asked softly.

"No." Zoe moved to the bathroom and he followed. Zoe unfolded a towel on the counter, then working over the towel, she unscrewed the lid and banged the bottle on her palm a few times until she felt the first stone. The bracelet slipped into her hand covered in globs of lotion. She used the back of her fingers to wipe away some of the lotion, which revealed the facets of the diamonds, their sharp angles catching the light. She found the stone on the end and rubbed away the lotion, revealing the broken clasp.

Jack wiped his hand over his mouth. "That's real. That's it."

"I know," Zoe said with a sigh. "I hoped I was wrong—that I'd made a mistake, and it would look like an imitation. But this is it."

"Yes. Unfortunately, I think you're right."

"What are we going to do? Someone tried to frame us."

Still staring at the bracelet, Jack said, "I don't know, but I think the best thing would be to get you to the airport right away."

"Why? Can you think of someone I could take this to? Someone who'd help us out?"

"No, to get you out of here."

"I'm not going to go off and leave you here to sort this out on your own."

A faint smile turned up the corners of his mouth. "Don't think I can handle it on my own?"

"You are the most resourceful person I know, but I'm not

leaving you to deal with this by yourself. We do things together, not on our own. We work better that way."

"Zoe, you should go now, while there's the chance."

"No. We're not going our separate ways. We're all in on this marriage thing, so I'm not running away at the first hint of trouble."

"The first hint of trouble would have been that quarrel we had last year over where to put the new couch. This is in a different league."

"Doesn't matter. All in. Not leaving."

He stared at her a moment then blew out a sigh. "For someone with such a free and easy personality you can be quite obstinate."

"All part of my charm." She kissed him on the cheek. "Thank you for not being too absurdly old-fashioned about it."

"Yes, well. I'm not sure that's a compliment, but in any case," he pointed to the bottle, "I think we should get out of here and find a safe place for that. There's no guarantee that Alessi won't come back and search our room again."

"Sounds like a good plan. I don't want to stick around here anyway."

5

THEY LEFT THEIR ROOM, BUT didn't return their key to the nook in the wall behind the unmanned front desk. They'd decided that, for now, the lotion bottle was the best place for the bracelet. The lotion certainly wouldn't harm the diamonds, and it wouldn't be unusual for Zoe to carry a small bottle of it.

"Are they still with us?" Zoe asked.

"Bun Lady has dropped back, and Mustache Guy is on point."

"Great. Where are we going?"

"Someplace busy and noisy. I know just the place."

They twisted through the streets, stopping to admire windows where Zoe didn't look at anything on display, only the reflection of the people in the glass. Their two followers stayed with them. Zoe was so focused on what was happening behind them that she barely paid attention to where they were going, but as they moved through increasingly crowded streets, Zoe heard the rush of water. "What is that?"

Jack smiled fleetingly, the first break in his grim expression since they'd left Alessi. "Wait and see."

"That's not the Trevi Fountain, is it? It is," she said as they rounded a corner and emerged into a cozy piazza where the roar of water was even louder, and tourists stood fifteen deep in front of the famous landmark. A mass of twisting mythical figures, the fountain centered on Oceanus, who looked bulky and a bit like a WWF fighter as he rode his shell-like chariot, pulled by two powerful sea horses, which were flanked by tritons. The reverberation of the flowing water filled the space. "Impressive. And a great idea." Zoe worked her way down the shallow steps to the edge of the pool at the base of the fountain. Even over the roar of the water, Zoe heard chatter in English, French, Italian, German, and possibly Russian. She fished some coins from her messenger bag and handed a few to Jack.

"You only need one," he said.

She tossed her coins. "Insurance," she said and then felt her smile falter as she remembered Harrington's quip about throwing coins in the fountain to insure he returned to Rome.

Jack nodded. "I know what you're thinking." He tossed his coins.

Oblivious of the other tourists edging forward to take their place, Jack held their ground at the edge of the fountain and looped an arm around Zoe's shoulders. "Now's a great time to talk. Can't be overheard and our friends are hovering at the top step."

"I don't even know where to start." Zoe rested her head against his shoulder for a moment, then pulled away to look at his face. "That theory of Alessi's about how the jewels were stolen—the sleight of hand thing—is the most absurd thing I've ever heard."

"I agree, but somehow, someway the switch was made."

"And we ended up with the bracelet. I suppose figuring out what to do with it is the most urgent thing." She ran through the thoughts she'd had in the bathroom when she first discovered it. "I considered telling Alessi I didn't know where it had come from, or how it got there but..."

"Considering they showed up expecting to find the jewels, I'm sure we would have been arrested, not just questioned and released. No, it was a good call to hide it, at least until we figure out what happened."

"Well, it wouldn't be hard to put it in our room," Zoe said. "Anyone could watch for us to leave, then slip in and get the key when the desk clerk was away."

"Which is often, apparently. We've retrieved our own key several times."

"And we were out this morning, so it could have happened then."

Zoe blew out a breath and focused on the water gliding across the flat surfaces of the fountain then sheeting over the edge into the pool. "But why leave one piece of the set in our room?"

"Simple. We take the blame for the theft, the police focus on us, giving the real thief time to unload the necklace and earrings. The bracelet is made of smaller stones, while the earrings were larger and matched, so more valuable. The necklace is the show-piece of the set and has the most stones. If they have to give up something, it might as well be the piece with the smaller stones. And it was easily identifiable as the stolen bracelet since the clasp was broken. This way, someone fingers us for the theft, but they still have the majority of the most valuable stones available to sell."

"But how could they do that? Won't it be...what do they call it in the movies...hot? The Flawless Set is already famous, and after all the publicity for the exhibit, even average citizens like me who don't know much about jewelry would recognize it. There have been ads and posters all over town for it, even one on the side of a bus."

"But if you sold the stones individually..."

"Break up the set? That would be terrible," Zoe said.

"No, that's how to make money."

"Right. We are talking about someone cold enough to steal the set in the first place, and then lay out a plan that would implicate us. It all had to be planned...the whole thing. The switch of the real jewels for fakes, and the hollowed out center of the plaque, as well as the placement of the bracelet in my jewelry bag."

"Yes, we were set up very neatly."

"Look, more police." Zoe tilted her head toward the edge of the piazza. The sunken fountain was positioned several steps below the main piazza. On the right and the left of the fountain, a low wall ran alongside the fountain, creating an amphitheater-like setting. Two police officers paced along the wall. Their higher elevation gave them a good view of the tourists crowding around below. As they scanned the crowd, Zoe gripped the messenger bag tighter, feeling the bump under the layers of leather where she'd tucked the lotion bottle.

"They're probably not looking for us." Jack's voice was calm, but his gaze bounced between the police officers and Mustache Guy, who had moved halfway down the steps.

"I wish we had somewhere safe that we could stash the lotion bottle. I don't suppose we could convince a bank to give us a safety deposit box?"

"Only if we want to show ID, and we'd probably have to have an Italian address, too."

"So that's out. What about Left Luggage? There's one at the Termini." Zoe had checked into baggage storage options because they'd arrived several hours before check-in on the day they flew into Rome, but their hotel had let them store their bags with them until their room was ready. "The drawback is we'll have to show our passports to drop it off and pick it up."

Jack frowned. "Not fond of that idea."

"I know. If Alessi figures out that we stored something there, he'll want it."

"And would probably be able to get whatever warrant or permission he needed."

"I suppose we could mail it to someone," Zoe said reluctantly. "But I hate to do that. No matter how good the tracking is, packages still get lost."

"And who would we mail it to?" Jack asked. "Whoever it is, we'd pull them into this mess as well."

"I don't like the idea either." Zoe's forehead wrinkled into a frown. "There's Nico, I suppose." Nico was an old friend from Jack's consulate days in Naples. Jack had recruited Nico as an asset because of Nico's family connections with the Comorra, the powerful Naples mafia. Nico's fun-loving, Lothario exterior hid a shrewd mind, and he had helped Jack and Zoe out of a few serious scrapes. They'd had dinner with Nico the day after they arrived in Rome. He had become quite the globetrotting entrepreneur, and Rome had been on his itinerary frequently because his fiancée lived there.

Jack actually laughed. "Now, that would be a dangerous place to leave it."

"You're right. The temptation would probably be too great, but I can't think of anything else."

Jack said, "There is one other option, if it's still open, but we need to lose our escorts."

"I'm up for both of those things." Zoe felt as if the lotion bottle were pulsing and glowing, sending out signals to come and find it. "The police are coming down the steps, too. Time for us to leave, I think."

Mustache Guy was inching his way through the crowd toward them. With the steps blocked, Zoe and Jack pushed through the tourists at the edge of the fountain, trying to reach the far end of the left side of the fountain, but the tourists weren't about to give up their prime viewing spots.

Zoe turned and scanned the crowd in front of Mustache Guy. She spotted a tall man with thick salt-and-pepper hair and sunglasses. She pointed as she shouted, "Hey, isn't that George Clooney?"

A beat of silence followed as people around her turned, following her pointing finger, then the crowd of tourists surged toward the man in the sunglasses. Mustache Guy was caught in the flow. As the tourists jostled for a better look at the "movie star," Jack and Zoe cut through the crowd, scrambled over the low wall, and raced across the piazza to one of the tight streets that branched off from it.

Zoe focused on not tripping over the curb or the uneven cobblestones as they sprinted. They were moving so quickly that she couldn't look back. They dodged between pedestrians for several blocks. Jack slowed, and Zoe realized they were on the Via del Corso, one of the best shopping streets in Rome with lots of high-end stores that ran in a straight line into the heart of Rome. Ahead, at the end of the street, she could see the Victor Emmanuel monument, the massive, blindingly white monument the locals called the Typewriter.

Jack looked back. "Mustache Guy is still with us."

As they left the confines of the street and burst into the open area with a traffic circle in front of the monument, Zoe glanced back. "I see Bun Lady, too."

"Come on." Jack caught her hand, and they ran toward the monument. With flights of stairs, rows of columns, flags, fountains, and statues of horses, chariots, and goddesses, all layered and stacked together, the whole thing felt overdone. They'd walked by it earlier in the week after their visit to the Forum, and Zoe didn't even glance at it as they made for an idling bus.

They shoved on with the group of waiting commuters and tourists, losing Mustache Guy, but Bun Lady hopped on at the last second. Jack nodded toward the front of the bus, and they worked their way forward until they were near the front exit. At the next stop, they were the first ones off and were several steps away when Jack said, "Backtrack. Act like you forgot something."

They doubled back, and Jack bumped into Bun Lady, who was only a few steps behind them. The impact with Jack's shoulder sent her tottering across the sidewalk away from the bus into a cluster of students. Zoe's hand clasped the bus handrail inside the open doors, and she hopped onto the bottom step of the stairwell, the only open space on the packed bus. She felt Jack push in behind her seconds before the doors closed behind him. The bus lumbered away, and Zoe's gaze connected with the woman's as she untangled herself from the students.

———

Nigel came out of his office, grabbed a rolling chair from a nearby empty desk, and pulled it alongside Gemma's desk. "That tip on the country home robberies come to anything?"

She swiveled toward him, her golden eyebrows pinched together in a frown. "No. Terrance Croftly is so clean I'm surprised he doesn't sparkle."

Nigel raised his eyebrows. "So you're saying he's a vampire?"

Gemma laughed. "Pop culture point for you. No, he's definitely human, an ordinary one, at that. "No record. Not even a hint of illegal activity. Doesn't associate with any known criminals. Not even a parking ticket. Model citizen, by the looks of it. He trained under his uncle, the original owner of the store. Terrance bought him out last year."

"Hmm. And yet, there's the tip about the cross."

"And yet." She sighed. "I'm beginning to wonder if the informant just made it up."

"Hell of a thing to make up though—a medieval cross."

"I know," Gemma agreed. "Why not just say it was diamonds or miscellaneous gems? A medieval cross is specific, which makes me think there's something to it." Nigel nodded in agreement.

She waved a hand at the computer. "I'm checking some of his social media. He's got a few accounts—Facebook, Twitter, Instagram—but I don't see anything that I can pursue."

"Well, we can consider setting up a sting when you get back."

"Back?"

"From Rome. If you want to go." Nigel put a folder on her desk. "The Flawless Set has been stolen from an exhibit in Rome. Heard of it?"

"Hasn't everyone? It's as famous as the Hope Diamond."

"Right. The anonymous owner, who happens to be a citizen of Great Britain, has requested Scotland Yard look into it. I figured you're already working gems, I'd see if you wanted in on this one. If you don't want it, I'll send Davy."

"Are you kidding?" Gemma grabbed the folder. "It's Rome. I'm going home to pack."

6

A LESSI STUBBED OUT HIS CIGARETTE in the crystal ashtray on the desk without looking away from the papers he gazed at, giving the impression that he was completely absorbed in them. He wasn't interested in the papers at all. They were simply a few notes jotted during one of the recent interviews. Alessi was not a man to take notes. That was a duty for Bernando, who sat in the corner of the room with his tape recorder and notepad. No, Alessi didn't care about the papers. He was interested in the young woman seated on the far side of the desk. Making her, or any witness, wait revealed several interesting things. Even with his focus on the desk, he had been aware of her careful, almost hesitant movements as she came in and took a seat. And now the quick rise and fall of her chest showed she was nervous. Of course, most people would find a Carabinieri interview intimidating.

Without raising his head, he asked, "Name and position with Millbank and Proust?"

"Amy Beck," she whispered. "Assistant to Mr. Throckmorton."

He quickly ran through the rest of the details, her address in

London, phone number, and the day she arrived in Rome. Her answers were almost inaudible.

"Now, Signorina Beck," he said, finally raising his head. "Why did you not point out the fake last night instead of this morning?"

"What?" Her brown eyes widened and her forehead wrinkled.

"The substitution was made last night. Why did you not point it out then?"

"I didn't notice it. I didn't actually go near it last night. That was Mr. Throckmorton's job. To secure it, make sure everything was done properly."

"But you are his assistant."

"Yes," she agreed, somewhat reluctantly.

"So you would have been aware of his plans to switch the real jewels with the fakes."

"No—no. Mr. Throckmorton would never—"

Alessi overrode her words, his volume growing louder. "But how could you not be? You have access to all his correspondence, do you not? His phone, his computer, you manage that sort of thing for him. That is what assistants do, isn't it?"

She swallowed hard, shaking her head. "No. No, there was nothing. Nothing like that at all," she said, bursting into tears.

Alessi sat back and watched her shaking shoulders for a moment. She was nothing like the feisty redhead, he thought. That one had been a fighter. This one was weak. Easily played.

Between sobs, she said, "I knew something like this would happen. Mrs. Davray said not to be silly, that no one would suspect me, but you think I knew, that I helped him." She sniffed and wiped her nose on the back of her hand. "But I didn't. I promise I didn't." She gazed at him beseechingly with her large brown eyes, now rimmed in smudged black. "I only went to work for Mr. Throckmorton a few months ago, anyway. I've barely learned my way around the offices back in London."

Alessi pushed a tissue box across the desk. "Tell me exactly what you did last night."

Hesitantly, she reached out for a tissue, then quickly snatched one as if Alessi was a dangerous animal she shouldn't get too close to. She ran the tissue under her eyes. "I spent most of the night at the door, checking guests in. When Mr. and Mrs. Andrews arrived, I walked them back to the final room of the exhibit."

"And why was that?"

She had relaxed a bit and blew her nose, a great honking sound, before continuing, "Mr. Throckmorton told me to."

"And did you know why he wanted them in that room, especially?"

"No."

"Did you ask?"

"No."

Alessi repressed a sigh. His job would be so much easier if people were less like sheep and more inquisitive.

"And you didn't think it odd?"

"No," she said simply. "Why should I?"

Alessi reached for another cigarette. "And the plaque—where was it before the presentation?"

"Under a table at the back of the room."

"Who gave it to Signora Davray? You?"

"Yes, but...well, I went to get it, but Mr. Throckmorton already had it out. He gave it to me to give to her right before the presentation."

"Was this before or after the jewels went into the case?"

"After, I think."

A tap on the door sounded. Alessi barked, "Sì?" Amy jumped.

A man entered and handed Alessi a note. It read, "Lost Andrews and wife."

Alessi jumped up, let out a string of Italian. Amy slid lower in the chair.

———

Jack and Zoe rode the bus to the Termini, went in, and circled around for a while until Jack was sure there wasn't anyone else on their tail. "Where to now?"

Jack gestured to her messenger bag. "Now we go drop some luggage."

Zoe gripped the bag. "Oh, no. We're not dropping this off. This is my new bag. My other one, I lost in Venice, if you remember. I'm not losing this one."

"Fair enough." Jack grinned. "We can buy luggage from a street vendor."

Jack led the way out of the Termini, and they stopped at a kiosk with scarves, knock-off purses, and tote bags as well as tiny rolling bags, which were about the size of rolling suitcases with cartoon characters on them that she'd seen kids toting through the airport in the States. "Everything is scaled down in Europe, cars, trucks, living space, even the suitcases," Zoe mused as they purchased the smallest suitcase and a felt blanket to fill up the space. She put the lotion bottle inside the roll of the blanket and zipped the suitcase up. "Okay, what's this other option?"

"This way." Jack turned north. After several blocks, he nodded to a self-serve laundry tucked between a bakery and a pizzeria. Under the larger sign for the laundry, a smaller one stated, "Deposito Bagagli."

Inside, they passed by two student-types loading clothes from enormous backpacks into the machines. At the back counter, a young Indian man greeted them and explained in a mix of Italian peppered with English that he could take their bag and store it for seven days. He had Zoe sign the portion of the numbered tag, which he attached to the suitcase handle then he tore off the stub, pointing to a blank line at the bottom of the stub, then to the signed tag. "Sign when you return. Must match."

Zoe nodded that she understood, and Jack paid the man in advance for seven days. "I hope we don't need to leave it that long."

"But better safe than sorry," Zoe agreed.

The man smiled and dipped his head in a slight bow as they completed the transaction, then wheeled the suitcase to a door behind the counter, which he unlocked. As they moved away, Zoe caught a glimpse of a narrow room lined with shelves with numbers thumbtacked to the edges. The man lifted their suitcase into an open slot on the top shelf.

"Let's hope sixty-four is our lucky number." Zoe put the ticket stub in the folder that held her passport. The creamy leather folder had been a bon voyage gift from Helen. It had a section sized for her passport on one side; slots for credit cards were on the other side. Zoe inserted the stub deep into one of the credit card slots where it couldn't be seen at first glance.

Jack checked the street through the large plate glass window before holding the door open for her. Zoe looked pointedly at the simple lock on the front door. "You're sure this place is secure enough?"

"Yes. This is our best bet." Jack raised his eyes to the awning covering the storefront where a steel grate hung in a neatly retracted roll. "They lower that at night and there's no back entrance. I heard about this place back when I worked in Naples. A few people at the Consulate used it for storage if they had a few extra hours in Rome. Shorter lines than at Left Luggage at the Termini, and it's secure. I'm just glad it's still open."

"Well, at least I'm not carrying it on me." Zoe felt like the messenger bag was ten pounds lighter.

"Next up, finding Harrington." Jack dialed his number then shook his head. "Still not answering."

"So unlike him. But how do we even go about finding him? Alessi said Harrington wasn't in his hotel room. I wonder if Alessi checked the hospitals?"

"I'm sure it's on his list. I hope he's running down the whereabouts of everyone who was at the exhibit last night."

"Too bad we're at the top of that list. I get the feeling he's more focused on us than anyone else."

"Yes. He thinks we did it, but he can't afford not to investigate everyone, which may give us some breathing room, at least for a while. I'd like to see Harrington's hotel room."

"Isn't that risky?"

"What's this? *You*, worried about risk? You like risks and a bit of danger."

"Only when it involves rollercoasters and rock climbing, not breaking and entering. That's just crazy."

"Who said anything about breaking and entering? Remember, I'm stodgy and cautious," he said with a grin.

"You're never going to let me forget that, are you?" Before she'd sussed out Jack's secrets, she'd thought he was a dull, average sort of guy, which, after her crazy, unsecure upbringing, had actually appealed to her. Initially, she'd liked the safety and security she felt with Jack, the plodding, ordinariness of his life. But then one day the ordinary became irritating. What first appealed to her became the thing that annoyed her the most, his stick-in-the-mud lifestyle, marked by caution and carefulness. What she hadn't understood was that Jack's past was anything but ordinary. "Maybe I thought that once, but I know deep down, you're a thrill-seeker. You just hide it well."

They'd been walking along the street, and Zoe hadn't missed that while they were walking and talking, Jack constantly checked the area around them, surveying the crowds. The smile left her face as they reached the Termini. "So, it has to be Harrington's hotel room?"

"Have you got a better place to start?"

Zoe thought for a second. "The Hotel Santa Maria, wasn't it?"

Zoe consulted her *Smart Travel* Rome guidebook and was relieved to see the Hotel Santa Maria was listed. It was located near the Spanish Steps, so they caught the Metro at the Termini and rode it to the Spagna stop, then took the elevator to the top of the steps, which was not nearly as scenic as climbing the actual steps, but they weren't sightseeing today. They emerged at the top of the steps near the obelisk and made their way through a cluster of artists displaying their canvases and only paused for a second to take in the view down the steps, then continued on to the Via Sistina, one of the constricted streets of hotels, restaurants, and shops that branched off the piazza. The sun was high and bright in the sky, but with the tall buildings on either side, the street was shady. The Hotel Santa Maria was about halfway down the street with several police cars, including a Carabinieri car, parked in front of its revolving glass door. A couple of business-suited men carrying briefcases chatted on the red carpet outside the hotel.

Zoe and Jack slowed their pace as they neared the hotel. He looked across the façade of the building. "Okay, four floors. We go inside, act like we know where we're going and take the stairs or the elevator, if they have one. I'm betting a hotel this posh has an elevator. Once we're on the floors with the rooms, we stroll, looking for Harrington's."

Zoe eyed the police cars. "You think his room will be obvious."

He nodded. "Once we find out where it is, then we figure out how to get in."

"It's a good plan, but I don't like the idea of traipsing along hallways and accidentally running into the police. Since, you know, we were just running from them."

They stopped walking, and Zoe pretended to consult her map. Jack leaned over it, too. "Do you have another idea?"

"As a matter of fact, I do." Zoe looked pointedly at two women in maid uniforms leaving the building through a small door cut into another larger door a few feet from the hotel's main entrance. "I bet they know everything that's going on in the hotel—where the police are, what they've found, and what was going on in the rooms before the police arrived."

Huddled close over the map, Jack turned to look at her, his face close to hers. "You're too good at this, sometimes."

"I've learned from the best." She put away the map, and they followed the women to a café down the street where the women bought slices of pizza.

Zoe nodded to a souvenir store across the street. "I'll wait here. One person is less memorable than two."

"Good idea. Now, all I have to do is drag some Italian out of my memory banks." He took the map, and Zoe went to browse T-shirts and refrigerator magnets. She watched him enter the café and approach the table, map in hand. He fixed his silver-blue gaze on the women, and even from across the street, Zoe could see him turn on the charm.

The women seemed eager to help, hands flying as they talked. Zoe smothered a smile. Worried about his Italian. Right. All he had to do was smile and those women were eating out of his hand. Zoe turned her attention back to browsing, stepping aside as a woman entered the store and made for the cash register at the back. The store was tiny, little more than two rows of shelves on each side and a cash register at the back. Zoe immediately recognized the woman who'd entered the store was Harrington's flustered assistant. The rolling bag she pulled behind her bumped one of the shelves and sent a stack of T-shirts sliding.

"So sorry—oh."

"Amy, isn't it?" Zoe asked as she grabbed the T-shirts before they hit the floor.

"Yes. Um..." A sales person, a girl in her late teens, came out from behind the cash register, frowning.

"Zoe. From the exhibit." They stepped back and the sales girl replaced the shirts.

"Right. Sorry. I'm just so scattered. With everything that's happened—I just wanted a shirt. I have to get something before I leave Rome."

"You're leaving?"

"Yes. I can't wait to get out of this city. I thought that horrid little detective or inspector, or whatever he is, wasn't going to let me leave. He actually said we all had to stay." Her hair slipped over her face and she pushed it behind her ear with fingers that shook. "As if Mrs. Davray would stand for that. Mrs. Davray told him that she is not going to miss her flight this afternoon. And Mr. Goccetto has been gone for hours anyway."

"Really?"

"Yes. He caught some late flight last night after the exhibit so it is completely unreasonable to expect the rest of us to stay. It's not like we know anything." She heaved a sigh. "If only Mr. Throckmorton were here, he would have sorted everything out. I'm on holiday today. My mum's expecting to pick me up at the airport this afternoon. It's the first holiday I've had since going to work for M&P, and if Mr. Throckmorton were here, there wouldn't even be a question. He'd see that I got to leave. Of course, Mrs. Davray did too," she added reluctantly, "but with her, it's more of an accident that it happened. Mr. Throckmorton would remember that I was on holiday and make sure I got it."

"And Harrington? Where's he?"

"No one knows." Her eyes widened. "Not like him at all. He's never rude. He always returns calls and never misses a meeting. People are whispering..." She lowered her voice then suddenly seemed to remember something and flushed. "Never mind. Sorry, I shouldn't have said anything. We're not supposed to talk to anyone. About any of it," she added miserably. "I just forgot. You were at the exhibit and all..." she trailed off.

The sales girl held up one of the shirts with an Italian flag on it.

"Um..." Amy pushed her flyaway hair out of her eyes. "No. Do you have one with the Colosseum on it? Yes? Oh, good. Yes. I'll take it. Small. Little." Amy held her hands a few inches apart.

The three of them did a little dance, moving around so that the sales girl and Amy could get to the back of the store where Amy paid.

"Well, goodbye," Amy said as she passed Zoe on her way out.

"Have a good flight." Zoe browsed the T-shirts then decided she needed to move along. As she turned to leave, she saw Amy had left several papers and an airline ticket on the counter by the cash register.

Zoe snatched them and sprinted to the sidewalk. Amy was already almost to the piazza where a rank of taxis waited. Zoe jogged up the street and caught her just as she glided into one of the taxis while the driver held the door.

An expression of alarm chased across Amy's face as she turned to Zoe, her eyes sharp and wary, but then almost instantly the expression was gone, replaced by a limpid half-questioning gaze. "You forgot this." Zoe held out the papers and the ticket.

"Oh, thank you. I would have—I don't know what I would have done—"

Zoe cut off her stammering thanks. "You're welcome. Better get going." She stepped back and the driver slammed the door then moved to his own seat. The taxi tore down the street and Zoe followed slowly.

Jack met her coming up the street. "You look contemplative."

She recounted her meeting with Amy as they walked toward the Spanish Steps. "She looked so scared. I guess that's what is bothering me. She looked like she wanted to get away as fast as she could. I wonder...do you think she knows something and isn't letting on? I don't usually scare people."

"She might know something. It's possible. On the other hand, you can be quite intimidating, especially before you've had your coffee."

Zoe jabbed him playfully on the arm. "This is serious. Well, no way to know now. She's gone. Did you find out anything?"

"The maids said there's nothing in Harrington's room."

"So he's gone. Just like Carlo."

"What? Your admirer has left town?"

"He's not my admirer."

"He was taken with you. I practically had to use a wedge to join your conversation."

"Don't blame me. You were the one who sent me on that errand. He's one of those men who has to 'conquer' every woman in his sphere, at least in his own mind. Tiresome, really."

"Can't say I'm sorry that he left town, though. Where did he go?" Jack asked as they reached the steps and began the descent.

"She didn't say. Speaking of charming women, I saw you working your brightest smile on the maids. You must have found out something else."

"The police have Harrington's room blocked off, but the maid saw it this morning before they arrived. It's in the same state as it has been for the last several days. Empty."

"Empty, as in he wasn't staying there?"

Jack nodded. "She said the bed hadn't been slept in—for days—and there was no trash. No clothes in the closet, no suitcase, no toiletries."

"Then he had to be staying somewhere else. He did say he visited here often. Maybe he's staying with a friend."

They both stopped. "The pink building—," Zoe said.

Jack finished her thought. "The one by the Pantheon."

7

THE TAXI DROPPED THEM AT the Pantheon. They went
to the little café where they had talked with Harrington
then retraced their steps through the streets. "Both times he asked
us to meet him, it was near here. It makes sense that he stayed
somewhere around here. Otherwise, why not ask us to meet him
near the Spanish Steps?"

"He could just be extremely cautious. He wanted to meet with
us away from the hotel where the insurance employees were staying. That fits with his personality."

"But when we made plans with him last night, it wouldn't have
mattered if we were seen with him today. The opening is over, and
there is no secret to keep about our being in touch with him now.
We could have met near the Hotel Santa Maria. This is a long way
to go in the heat," Zoe said, glad an enormous cloud had drifted in
front of the sun, which dropped the temperature a couple of
degrees.

They made a few false turns before they found the pink building. A woman was entering through a small cutout inside the

larger double green doors, and they hurried forward to catch the miniature door before it closed completely.

"Jack, wait." Zoe stopped to look at the list of names beside the buzzers on the wall by the front door. "Look at Number Ten."

Jack stepped back, but held the door open with one hand. Beside the buzzer for apartment ten was the name, *Morton*. It had been scribbled on a piece of paper and taped over the last occupant's name. Every other name was obviously Italian. "Short for Throckmorton, possibly?" Zoe asked.

"Could be a coincidence," Jack said. "An English friend who happens to live in Rome."

Number Ten was on the top floor. The stairwell was quiet. The woman who'd entered before them had gone into a ground-floor apartment. Windows on each landing were open, but as they ascended, the heat intensified. They reached the top landing, and Zoe went to Number Ten, the only apartment on that floor and knocked.

Silence.

They exchanged a look. Jack banged on the door. "Harrington? It's Jack and Zoe. We need to talk to you."

After a minute more of silence, Jack tried the doorknob, but it didn't give. "We have to make sure..." He lifted the mat in front of the door then dropped it back into place. "No key here."

Zoe glanced around the bare landing. "There's nowhere to hide a key out here."

Jack ran his hands lightly along the top of the doorframe. "He could be in there, hurt or sick. It's the only explanation I can think of for his no show. You know he's not the type to forget appointments or ignore phone calls." Jack moved to one of the windows on the landing and repeated the process of checking around the frame, then bent to look under the sill.

Zoe sighed. "You're right. I can't see him forgetting us, or blowing us off either." She went to the window on the opposite side of the landing. It overlooked a cobblestoned courtyard filled with hatchbacks and Smart cars. Multi-story buildings with shutters thrown back and laundry fluttering in the breeze ringed the courtyard. She dutifully patted the frame, but didn't find anything, then leaned out the open window and looked to the right, toward the windows of apartment Number Ten. Zoe switched her messenger bag around so that it was positioned against her back, and after a quick glance around the courtyard to make sure no one was watching her, she threw a leg over the windowsill. "I've found it."

"The key?"

"No. Our way in." Zoe put her foot on the narrow decorative stucco ledge that ran along the building under the window, then pivoted on the ball of her foot as she pulled her other leg over the sill. Jack turned. "Zoe just because you rock climb in a gym in Dallas..."

Gripping the window frame and the shutter, she inched along. She reached around a drainpipe and grabbed the shutter of the next window with her left hand. She leaned into it slightly. It held firm. "Hush, Jack. You'll have everyone looking out their windows."

"I don't care. This is crazy. Do you know how far up you are?"

"No. You know why?" Zoe asked in a soft, abstracted voice as she edged her foot along the ledge then smoothly transferred it around the drainpipe. "Because when you're climbing, you focus on what's around you. Your next handhold, the next foothold." She shifted her right hand to the shutter and eased her body to the left, closer to the window, which was made of two narrow panes that ran the length of the opening vertically. They closed in the middle, but the latch wasn't fastened.

Zoe pushed gently on the windowpane closest to her left hand.

It swung inward. She inched closer and peered inside. The apartment was small enough that in one quick glance she could see there was no one home. She carefully transferred her grip from the shutter to the window frame and lightly hopped into the room, which was a mixture of the traditional lines of the building with moldings and ornate light figures combined with the contemporary accents. She recognized the flower prints hanging on the wall from her IKEA browsing.

She stepped down over a pale blue couch, which was paired with a floral print chair and positioned in front of a glass coffee table. Across the room, a desk was positioned beside the window that looked out on the street.

The back half of the apartment was divided between a kitchenette and a bedroom. All Zoe had to do was lean slightly to the side to see the bedroom was also uninhabited. The bed, its white duvet cover smooth and unwrinkled, took up most of the space, but a small round table had been wedged along one side of it and served as a nightstand with a clock and lamp. A freestanding double-door closet in white pressboard, one of those do-it-yourself assembly jobs that came in a flat-pack box, took up the rest of the room. The door to the bathroom stood open, showing tiny octagon tiles covering the floor, a pedestal sink, and a modern shower insert. Laminated pieces of paper were positioned around the apartment with instructions in several languages. There was one by the coffee machine and another by a radiator.

She went to the front door, checked to make sure there wasn't an alarm, then swung it open, noticing that there was another laminated card by the door with instructions on how to find the building's laundry room.

Jack stood on the threshold, breathing hard. "Zoe, that was a crazy, dangerous stunt."

"I was perfectly safe. Just because you don't like climbing—"

"It has nothing to do with what I like or don't like. I wasn't the one out there."

"Precisely. I knew you wouldn't want to do it, so I did."

"No, you knew I wouldn't *let* you do it."

Zoe leveled a look at him. "I don't think we want to go there right now, do we? Are you coming in or not? No matter how hard you searched, we weren't going to find a key out there, and short of you picking the lock—and this one looks sturdy—that was our only way in. You wanted in. We're in."

Jack said something as he stepped inside that Zoe pretended not to hear. He shut the door with his elbow and quickly looked in the bedroom and bath.

"There's no one here. I checked." Zoe went directly to the desk. "This apartment must be a temporary rental. There are instructions all around the place. Here's one by the phone, and the first number listed is for Rome Holiday Vacation Rentals."

Jack paused to read the laminated note by the radiator. "Looks like it."

"It does look like Harrington is staying here." She pointed to a stack of business cards with his name. "And look, paperwork from Millbank and Proust." Zoe indicated several sheets of what looked like inventory lists printed on forms with the company name at the top and Harrington's signature at the bottom.

"Don't touch anything." Jack handed her a kitchen towel. "First order of business. Let's get rid of your fingerprints." He went to the door and wiped down the doorknob and the frame.

Zoe's thoughts skipped from Alessi's questions about the plaque to the news that Harrington's room hadn't been used at the hotel—that odd fact would stand out to Alessi, and he had more resources than they did. It wouldn't be long before Alessi connected this room with Harrington, especially if Harrington had paid for it with a credit card.

Zoe wiped down the window glass and the frame, not an easy feat, considering she had to use her shoulder to hold the window steady. When she was sure it was clean, she turned her attention back to the room. Jack was occupied at the desk, using a pencil to move around papers. He tapped a stack of folders he'd fanned out across the desk with the pencil eraser. "Look at this."

She angled her head so she could see the names on the tabs. One seemed to leap out at her. "London Premiere," she read aloud. "As in, the jewel heist at the London movie premiere?"

"I think so," Jack said with a grim note in his voice. "You take these." Zoe managed to maneuver the folders into the dishtowel without touching them with her bare hands and went to sit on the couch. Using the towel as a glove, she clumsily went through the folders. The first was labeled, "Rowen Meadows," and contained several pages of official Millbank and Proust paperwork with specifics on a policy that covered several unique pieces of jewelry. Detailed descriptions as well as photographs were included of an exquisite peacock brooch. The main stone, the body of the peacock, was a heavy opal, a swirl of iridescent blue and green. Sapphires, emeralds, and diamonds studded the delicate gold tail and more diamonds and sapphires were positioned in the shape of the bird's neck and head. A history sheet described the origin of the stones, the jeweler who created the piece, and previous owners. The brooch was the most unusual piece, but it wasn't the most valuable. A ruby and diamond bracelet as well as a pink-hued diamond ring were given the same comprehensive treatment.

In comparison to the glossy photos, the rest of the file should have been boring, just hand-printed pages of notes about Rowen Meadows, the country home where the owner kept the jewels. Zoe found herself scanning each page, though, her heartbeat inching up as she read about security systems and codes, routines of household staff, and, lastly, maps of each floor of the house. Unlike the first pages of the file, which had been official documents from Millbank and Proust, the pages at the end were handwritten in what looked to be Harrington's distinctive, precise printing.

"The files you've got, are they about robberies?" Zoe asked, breaking the silence.

"One is. There was a robbery at Gilbrand House. Official documents and photographs of a medieval cross and several modern pieces with amethysts and garnets. At the back of the file, there are notes and maps about security in Gilbrand House."

"Hand-printed and meticulous?" Zoe asked.

"Yes." Jack scrubbed a hand over his face and muttered, "I didn't believe it—that he could be involved, but these files..."

"I know," Zoe said, swallowing at the devastated look on his face. "I'm sorry, Jack."

He raised his head, a bleak look on his face. "These are blueprints for robberies, with most of the incredibly sensitive information in Harrington's handwriting, or at least it looks like his handwriting to me."

"Me, too," Zoe said miserably. "It's such exact printing, and the slashes through the letter 't' with an upswing going from low on the left to high on the right, well, it looks like the 't' in his signature. And the loop on the 'g', isn't closed either, just like his note."

She flipped to the last file, the "London Premiere." It was slightly different. It had sketchier details on the jewels themselves, but the information on where the jewels would be stored and how they would be transported to the movie premiere was thick and copious. It was the only file with printouts of news articles that described how the jeweler's courier had been robbed inside his hotel room before he could transfer the jewels to the movie stars before they walked down the red carpet.

Zoe rubbed her forehead, hardly able to believe it. Harrington, the thief? It was so unlikely. But then again, Melissa Davray and Carlo Goccetto seemed utterly unlikely as well. It was hard to believe any of them were involved, but as Harrington had said, all it would take would be a partner.

"Zoe, there's more—a file about people," Jack said.

She went to look over his shoulder. "They're bios. Looks like they're from Millbank and Proust's website."

He used the pencil's eraser to flip through the pages with head-shots of Melissa Davray, Amy Beck, Carlo Goccetto, as well as two other men she didn't recognize. A short paragraph describing the person's background and their position at Millbank and Proust accompanied each photo. "Wait, slow down," Zoe said, noticing a few of the pages had the same squared off handwriting at the bottom.

"Dates and locations."

Zoe tapped her lip. "That one, February twenty-fifth. I just read something…" She turned and went back to the folders she'd been looking through. "Yes, that was the date of the robbery at Rowen House."

Jack flipped back and forth between the pages. "They all have the same list of dates, the dates of the robberies."

"He was…checking for alibis?" Zoe said. "He did it." She blew out a breath then put into words what they were both thinking. "He's the thief. The details, the planning, the notes. Why would he care about alibis?"

He went completely still. "What is it?" He was staring at the last paper in the folder.

It was a screen shot of Safe Haven's website home page. A printout of a newspaper article about the recovery of the lost art was stapled to the side along with a grainy photo of Jack, another screen shot, cropped to show only his face. Harrington must have pulled it off the web, from one of the articles about the fraud case.

"He wasn't checking alibis," Jack said. "He was looking for someone to pin the thefts on. He picked me."

"But you weren't even in Europe when those other robberies took place."

"No, but if Harrington managed to tie me to at least one, the Flawless Set, then the supposition would be that I was involved in the others, once the thefts were linked through Millbank and Proust. If you're going to go to the trouble of framing someone, it might as well be for all the thefts, right? Not just one. They might not have proof, but with my history..."

"Jack, this isn't good."

Jack spoke with his head in his hands. "I know. We're done."

"What?"

"Safe Haven is done. Everything Safe Haven is...it's all linked to Millbank and Proust, and Harrington, in particular. Our start-up money came from the finder's fee that Millbank and Proust gave us, which came through Harrington."

Melissa's words about ruining Safe Haven echoed in Zoe's head, but she pushed them away. "But no one—well, except the bank—knows where that money came from."

"But we got our first clients because of the return of the stolen art." Jack waved his hands over the folders. "And when it comes out that Harrington was involved in all these major thefts...we're done."

Zoe bit her lip then said, "Too bad there's not a fireplace in here." Jack looked at her then down at the files in front of him as she said, "but we could drop them in the river, or soak them in the shower until they're a soggy mess, then throw them away in some random trash bin. If we take them with us..."

"Too risky. If Alessi brings us in again before we have a chance to destroy them, it would be more incriminating evidence that he could use to make a case that we helped Harrington. Let's get them back exactly as they were."

"I don't like it," Zoe said as she reluctantly handed the towel-wrapped bundle back to Jack.

"Zoe, this is what we found on our own, in a few minutes of searching. Imagine what Alessi will be able to find with all the power of an official investigation—he's probably checking Harrington's bank accounts, credit cards, phone calls. Everything. Harrington could even have these same notes scanned and saved on a computer somewhere."

"That's true, but Harrington seems to avoid tech when he can. Alessi is probably searching our bank accounts and credit cards, too," Zoe said, gloomily.

"Probably," he agreed.

"At least our incredibly low bank balance will show him we're not lying. I doubt any thieves skate as close to being overdrawn as we do."

Jack laughed. "True. And we're using a burner phone, so that gives us a little extra time, too."

"So, we're unintentionally off the grid. I'm sure Alessi will interpret that in completely the wrong way."

"Only partially off grid. There's still the credit card charges for our hotel, but that's not going to matter. Once the word gets out that Safe Haven is linked to the theft of the Flawless Set, we're done."

"But we're innocent."

"Doesn't matter," Jack said flatly. "You know how things are spun. Once word gets out about Harrington, people will assume we were in it with him, helping him steal the Flawless Set, and from there, it's only a short leap to wondering if the whole thing—our company, you, me—if we're all complicit."

"That is crazy," Zoe said, but inside she felt a horrible sinking feeling. All they'd worked for, all Jack's hopes and dreams, smashed—and for a second time, too. "I think you're jumping to a conclusion."

Jack shook his head. "Sorry, but I'm not." He ticked the items off on his fingers. "We're here in Rome at the time of the theft. We've had meetings and communication with Harrington outside regular channels." Jack swallowed then said, "Harrington duped us. He cleverly set us up. The whole 'help-me-I-smell-a-rat-in-the-company' drew us in very effectively. If you hadn't been in the bathroom today and accidentally found the bracelet, we'd be in custody right now, assumed accomplices."

Zoe paced to the window then back to the desk, fisting her hands in frustration. She felt such a rush of anger at the whole situation. She had an urge to sweep the papers off the desk and scatter them around the room, but she fought it down. It wouldn't do any good. She blew out a calming breath instead. "Well, that's not what happened. And we're not going to sit around and be the patsies."

"I believe I'm the patsy here. Singular. Harrington only hired me."

"Yeah, we both know how well that will go over if the police find us. There's no way they'll believe I wasn't in on it. They won't parse it out into you and me, separately. We're in this together." Zoe strode to the window then swung around. "You know what we're going to do?"

A smile crept onto Jack's face. "I think that's a rhetorical question."

"You bet it is. You already know the answer. There's one way to make sure we don't go down for any of those thefts." She waved her hand at the folders. "You know what I'm going to say, right?"

"Yes, but I like this militant side of you."

She moved toward him.

"Okay, I'll say it," he said. "We find Harrington ourselves."

She nodded. "And the Flawless Set. If he doesn't have the jewels on him, he'll know where to find them. Then we turn Harrington and the jewels over to the police."

"Welcome to Roma, signora."

Gemma towered over the Italian officer by a good six inches. He introduced himself as Colonel Alessi. She wasn't sure what the protocol was for greeting a European business colleague. She'd traveled on business before, but it had always been to the States. She waited to see if he would commence with the European double cheek kiss, but he simply turned and led the way to his office where he gestured at a chair across from his desk.

After she left the office in London, Gemma had hurried back to her tiny basement flat, thrown some clothes in a suitcase, and headed for the airport. She'd caught a late afternoon flight and now, three hours later, had left the spitting drizzle of London behind.

Alessi slapped both hands on his desk and drew his chair forward. "Now, I will tell you what we know." He concisely outlined their theories about the robbery and how the investigation had proceeded. "We are focusing on three people, Harrington Throckmorton and a married American couple he gave an award to at the exhibit, a Jack and Zoe Andrews. On the morning the theft was discovered, we received a tip that they were all responsible. Throckmorton's disappearance and a plaque modified to smuggle the Flawless Set out of the opening that was presented to the couple, indicate we should continue to concentrate on them." He handed over a folder with a list of names and details. "The attendees at the exhibit and a summary of the interviews conducted so far."

Gemma scanned the list as Alessi went on to describe the hollowed-out plaque and their theory of how the Flawless Set had been stolen. "And there are no other suspects?" Gemma asked when he finished.

He shrugged. "There are always other suspects." He waved at the long list of attendees. "But for now, we concentrate on the three."

Gemma nodded. She knew all about prioritizing leads. She ran her finger down the list of names again, more slowly.

"You recognize a name?" Alessi asked.

She shook her head. "No, none of them jump off the page at me, but there's something...I can't quite figure out what it is." She had the sense that she'd seen one of the names before, but she couldn't place it. The vague feeling of familiarity hovered at the edge of her thoughts like an annoying gnat. She concentrated on each name, testing it, turning it over in her mind, but couldn't pin down the thought. She sat back. "I may have just read about one of these people in the papers in London—something like that."

A tap sounded on the door, and a young man hurried inside after Alessi called out for him to enter. As the younger man put some paper in front of Alessi and spoke hurriedly in Italian, he caught sight of Gemma and delivered the last of his information, his gaze fastened on her. He spoke so rapidly she couldn't understand a word. Alessi snapped out a few orders and shooed the man out of his office. He left, rubbernecking and smiling at Gemma. He nearly ran into the doorframe on his way out.

Alessi picked up a cell phone and made for the door.

Gemma jumped up. "Wait. Where are you going?" She grabbed her purse and followed him.

Alessi hurried down the hall. "Signor Throckmorton rented an apartment near the Pantheon," he said over his shoulder. He was moving so quickly that she only caught up with him outside the building as he reached for the handle of a dark blue sedan labeled with the word "Carabinieri" in white.

Gemma moved to the passenger side. "I'm coming with you." She had expected a bit of pushback—most investigators were territorial—and she was in Italy, where *machismo* wasn't exactly unheard of, after all. But she hadn't expected him to simply walk —no run—away from her.

She tensed for an argument, but he tipped his head to the side and waved her into the car. "Certainly."

He put on the lights and siren, gunned the engine, and slipped into a tiny opening between a delivery truck and a motor scooter. Gemma cringed, automatically swinging her feet to the side, as the motor scooter surged up to her door then braked hard, seconds before the impact.

"They always stop." Alessi raised his voice over the noise of the siren. "Romans are good drivers."

They would have to be, Gemma decided as she watched Alessi and several other Carabinieri cars, which had followed them, sweep in and out of traffic with casual abandon.

Alessi said, "You are surprised,"

"At the traffic?" Gemma asked.

"No, that I didn't leave you." Alessi shifted gears and powered around a slow moving hatchback.

"I thought you might not want me," she said candidly.

"Nigel sent you," he said, as if it settled everything. "I trust him, so I trust you." Gemma nodded. Of course, the two department heads would have met, probably at conferences over the years. "And," he raised his finger to emphasize his point, "you saw the stack of files on my desk, no? There is no end to the crime. I will take all the help I can get. I apologize for hurrying away from you.

When there is a good lead, it is all I see." He cupped one hand around his eyes like a blinder on a horse. "It is all that matters."

So not machismo, but pursuit of the case that had him leaving her in the dust, she thought and put it down to the passionate Italian nature. She couldn't imagine Nigel sprinting down the hall after a hot lead. He was about as likely to do that as he was to jump up in the middle of a meeting and dance a jig.

"But I will not forget you again," Alessi said.

"Good. Because I won't let you."

Alessi slowed down for a red light, checked the traffic, and then crossed the intersection.

"How much farther?" Gemma asked.

"Ten minutes more if we are lucky with the traffic."

8

"SO, I SAY BEFORE WE leave, we take the place apart." Zoe looked around the room, assessing it for possible hiding places.

"You think he hid the Flawless Set here?"

"Why not?" She looked pointedly at the files. "He obviously didn't think anyone would be looking around, or he would never have left those files out."

"True. Okay, I'll look at the rest of the desk."

"Then I've got the living room and the kitchen," Zoe said.

"First, I think we need something a little better than dishrags. There was a closet on the landing," Jack trailed off as he moved to the front door, opened it with the hem of his shirt, and slipped outside, leaving the door open. He returned in a few moments, wearing a pair of threadbare work gloves. He tossed a pair of rubber gloves to Zoe as he closed the door. "Storage closet, filled with cleaning supplies and a toolbox." He waved a pair of pliers and a screwdriver at her as he crossed back to the desk.

"Okay." She drew on the gloves. "But I hope we don't need to dismantle anything."

"Better to be prepared. I should have brought my backpack with me today."

"Because then you would have been vindicated for bringing duct tape on an international flight." After he was caught without certain tools of the trade that Jack needed on another trip, he had packed for this trip with all contingencies in mind. He'd said he didn't know exactly what Harrington wanted him to do at the exhibit and wanted to be prepared for all possibilities. Zoe wasn't exactly sure what he'd packed in his backpack, but knew his stash included binoculars, tools, and duct tape. The duct tape, in particular, had not gone over well at airport security.

"No, I had gloves in there," Jack replied in a slightly offended tone.

Zoe examined the chair and searched under the cushions. She moved to the couch and had just picked up one of the cushions when the faint slam of a door echoed through the building. Rapid footsteps pounded up the stairs. Zoe paused, the cushion suspended in the air and looked at Jack. "Harrington?" she whispered.

Jack had a drawer half-pulled out, but was frozen, listening as well. The footsteps grew louder.

Jack shifted quietly to the door, but the footsteps stopped. A door closed with a thud that shook the building. "That sounded like the floor below us," Zoe said.

"Yes," Jack agreed. "Probably just someone coming home from work."

Zoe nodded and they went back to their search, but this time they both had a single-minded focus and moved as quickly as they could. Zoe finished with the furniture and moved to the kitchen.

"Be sure to check under the drawers."

"I know how to search," she said. "I learned by searching for your hiding places," she reminded him

"Touché." He picked up the screwdriver and went to work, checking outlet covers.

The kitchen was small, and it didn't take Zoe long to move through the mostly empty drawers, cabinets, and refrigerator. Harrington was clearly a man who ate out. The only thing he seemed to use in the kitchen was the trashcan, which was filled with pizza boxes and take-out containers. As Zoe moved to the bathroom, she said, "What are we going to do if we don't find anything here? It makes sense he would want the Flawless Set close to him, but what if he did the opposite? What if it's in a safety deposit box, or what if he gave it to someone else? It might even be out of Italy for all we know."

"He'd have the same issues with opening a safety deposit box that we would. It's only been a short time since the exhibit, and Alessi is going to be looking into his every movement since then. Anything unusual will draw attention."

"But that's not going to help us find the Flawless Set." Zoe stepped out of the bathroom and moved to check the bedroom. "We can't trace his steps." She waved away a dust bunny from under the bed and sat back on her heels. "It looks like we're running out of options."

Jack stopped tapping baseboards. "I think we have to turn it around and go at the problem a different way." He pulled their burner phone from his pocket. "Reverse engineer it, so to speak."

Zoe opened the closet doors. "You mean, figure out the person Harrington will sell the jewels to?"

"Exactly."

"But that could be...anyone."

"No." Jack punched some numbers in his phone. "I bet there are only a handful of special—i.e. shady—dealers who handle 'merchandise' like the Flawless Set. Fortunately, we know someone who knows shady people."

Zoe's thoughts skipped over their list of friends and acquaintances. "Masard?" she asked, surprised that Jack would know the Parisian antique dealer's phone number off the top of his head. They'd met him last year when they'd run the missing artwork to the ground. "I don't know if he deals with jewelry much," Zoe said, thinking of Masard's shop crammed full of furniture and paintings.

Jack shook his head. "No, our *other* friend with shady connections."

Her face cleared. "Oh, Nico. Of course." She went back to looking through the closet. Nico was exactly the right person to call. They knew they could count on him to keep things quiet, and, despite his rather ridiculous manner, his knowledge of underground criminal dealings was vast.

Zoe finished with the closet and stripped the rubber gloves off her sweaty hands. Nothing. *It's not here*, she said to herself. The lack of discovery should have been disappointing, but there was something else, some important thought teasing at the edge of her mind that overrode the setback.

She stepped back, surveying the room as Jack's voice on the phone faded to a murmur. There was something off. She scanned the room again. If she could just concentrate, it would come to her...

Jack appeared in the doorway. "Nico says he'll ask around. We're going to meet him at his fiancée's apartment."

Zoe nodded in an abstracted matter and walked slowly into the living room, then snapped her fingers. "There's no suitcase."

"What?"

"The maid told you there was nothing in Harrington's hotel room, but there are clothes in the closet in the bedroom, so he was here. That cream-colored suit he wore when we met him at the Pantheon is in there. There's no mistaking it, so Harrington was staying here, but there's no suitcase here. Last night, after the exhibit, Harrington must have returned here, packed his suitcase, and left." Zoe rubbed her temple. "He took the jewels, and he could be anywhere. Some other hotel in Rome, or he might even have left Italy."

"Alessi will run down any travel, if Harrington charged it."

"But that won't do *us* any good. Maybe we could talk to the neighbors, see if he mentioned anything, a city or another hotel."

"Better if no one here notices us." Jack cocked his head to the side.

"Wait. The trash. There wasn't anything in the kitchen but empty food boxes, but the desk. Was there a trash can near the desk?" Zoe asked, already moving to the desk.

Jack didn't answer, but instead went again to the wall near the window that overlooked the street and carefully looked out, his back against the wall.

A trashcan was tucked into the footwell of the desk. Zoe fell on it as if it were a treasure chest, scrabbling through a few crumpled receipts and a couple of discarded letter-size pages. The receipts were all for food—pizza and coffee. Zoe flicked through the larger pages. The first ones were mostly blank with only a header or footer, and a few lines of text, the extra pages that print sometime at the tail end of a print job. A small printer rested on the corner of the desk. A laminated card with directions for its use was taped to the side, so Harrington must have had a laptop and printed some documents recently. The receipts had been on the bottom of the trashcan and were dated within the last two days. The printed pages had been on top of them.

"Zoe, we've got to go." Jack picked up the pliers and screw-driver from the edge of the desk and shoved them into his back pocket.

"What?" Zoe edged up to the window. She'd been so absorbed

in the papers that she hadn't been listening to the activity on the street, but there were Carabinieri cars parked directly in front of the building. An officer was already at the steps, speaking into the intercom, a blond woman in civilian clothes at his elbow.

Zoe flitted to the window on the other side of the room and looked into the courtyard. "There's a police car pulling in here, too."

Jack grabbed the rubber gloves from where she'd tossed them down on the back of the couch, gave the room another swift glance as the buzz indicating the release of the front door carried faintly through the building. Jack looked at Zoe. "They're in."

Zoe shoved the papers from the trash in the pocket of her shorts then reached out to open the windows. "We've got to go out this way."

Jack grabbed her elbow and pulled her back toward the front door. "No."

She planted her feet. "Jack, I know you don't like heights, but we have to. We can't stay in here, and they're coming up the stairs."

"You're right, we can't stay here, but if we go out that window, we'll be forced onto the roof."

"It's the only way—"

"No, not the only way. I climb with the speed of a sloth, which would slow you down and make us both vulnerable, but there's a bigger issue. Did you happen to notice if this building is connected to the next one? Will we be able to get across to the next building?"

"I don't know. I don't remember."

"I don't either." Using his shirttail to cover his hand, Jack opened the front door and listened. More than one set of feet pounded up the stairs.

"We can't go out that way," Zoe whispered.

"We're not going out. Yet." Jack listened for a second until there was a break in the footfalls, which meant they had reached a landing and were walking along the length of it to get to the next flight of stairs. As soon as the slam of feet on the steps stopped, Jack slipped out the door of the apartment, pulling Zoe with him. He closed the door silently behind them.

Zoe stifled a groan. "Now we're trapped. They'll just find us sooner." The rapid pounding of the feet on the stairs resumed as Jack propelled Zoe to a door across the landing. He whipped the closet door open, and motioned Zoe inside. She wedged herself between a vacuum cleaner and a mop. Jack squished in, and as he pulled the door closed, Zoe caught the flash of movement on the stairs in the tiny gap between the door and the frame before Jack closed it completely, and darkness enclosed them.

9

THERE IS ONLY SO LONG you can go without literally moving a muscle. Jack's back was pressed up against Zoe, and normally if they were in that position in complete darkness, she would have cuddled up and enjoyed it, but with every muffled sound from the other side of the door, she expected the door to be wrenched open. Eventually, Zoe moved a foot experimentally to the side and gently shoved a mass over an inch so she could move her leg and shift her messenger bag away from where it was digging into her hip.

"What are you doing?" Jack breathed.

"Moving. I have a cramp. We've been in here forever."

"Zoe, it's only been about ten minutes."

"Ten minutes without moving *is* forever, to me."

He chuckled softly. "If we time it right, we should be able to slip out soon."

Twice, he had eased open the door a few millimeters, but the door to the apartment stood wide open and several people, some in police uniforms, some in suits, trailed in and out, so Jack softly closed the door again.

One guy lounged against the banister and smoked a cigarette. Then it sounded like a new group of people trooped up the stairs. The small space was hot and stuffy and had a curious mixture of ammonia and dust that made Zoe feel like she was on the verge of sneezing. She fought off the urge as they listened to the cadence of feet on the stairs and the rapid bursts of Italian. There was a break in the sounds for about a minute.

"Third time's the charm, hopefully," Jack said, and a sliver of light cut into the darkness. "We're good. Ready?"

"I'm so ready." The words were barely out of her mouth before the door swung open. She blinked against the blinding light as they stepped out of the closet. The warm air of the upstairs landing washed over them, and it felt almost cool in comparison to the airless closet. Jack checked over the banister then gave a quick nod. Suddenly her fingers felt clumsy, but she managed to close the closet door silently then swung quickly around the post at the top of the stairs and trotted down beside him.

They met no one on the way down. As they reached the main floor and the door to the building, which was also propped open, letting in gusts of hot, dry air, Jack said, "Here we go. Try to keep your face down so they can't see it."

"Right." She flipped open her messenger bag and dug around it as though she were looking for something. Jack seemed to contract a sudden headache that required him to rub his forehead.

Zoe had no idea how many people or police cars were around the entrance to the building. She kept her gaze on the steps and then on the cobblestones. Everything else was just a blur of movement. Zoe and Jack paced quickly on, beyond the edge of the building, but it wasn't until they turned off the street into a smaller, shadowed canyon-like alley that some of the tension eased. "Good grief, that was terrible," Zoe said. "Next time we take the roof."

Nico's fiancée, Mara, lived in the fascist-inspired EUR neighborhood in the south of Rome that Mussolini designed. The severe, squared-off buildings looked boring and rather soulless compared to the heart of Rome with its ornate fountains, baroque buildings, and lively piazzas. The taxi dropped them in front of a grim apartment building. They made their way through the gray-tiled, echoing lobby to the elevator. As they rode to the twenty-third floor, Zoe put her hands in her pockets and felt paper crinkle against her knuckles. She pulled it out and opened it. "I forgot about this. I shoved it in my pocket when we realized the police were on the way up to Harrington's apartment."

Jack looked over her shoulder. "What is it?"

"Papers from Harrington's trash." She handed the receipts to Jack.

He quickly glanced through them. "They just show Harrington bought food and coffee around the apartment."

"I know, but look at this." Zoe pointed to a few lines of text on the top of one of the larger pages. "Driving directions. I think this is the last page of a hotel reservation. When you finish your reservation, there's a sheet to print with all the details of the reservation plus info on how to get there. Either Harrington decided he didn't need this page and threw it away, or he didn't realize it had the rest of the driving directions on it, and he tossed it by mistake. There isn't a final destination address, but we have the last few lines of driving instructions and a city is named. All we have to do is find out where this Lermoos place is on road B 187, and we'll know where Harrington was going."

"But that could have been printed anytime Harrington was staying there, or even before he came, if the cleaning service is lax."

"No, the receipts from the last few days were under it. This was thrown away after the receipts. And, there's a date on this page, too." She studied the fine print of the footer at the bottom of the page. "Printed yesterday." The elevator dinged, and the doors slid open. Jack stepped out of the elevator as Zoe reached for the button for the first floor. "We don't even need to talk to Nico now."

Jack put his hand out to prevent the door from sliding closed. "Yes, we do. The more information we have, the better."

Zoe shifted from one foot to the other. "Every second counts. Harrington has a huge head start on us. You know how Nico is. It will take forever to get out of there."

"I'll make sure we're not here too long. In and out. Fifteen minutes, tops. Nico has good connections. He's worth taking a few minutes to talk to."

Zoe sighed. "Sometimes I hate it when you're right. Especially when your logical method is the way to go."

"Your *carpe diem* method has its moments, too."

"Just not right now, I know." Zoe put the papers away and checked her watch as they exited the elevator. "Fifteen minutes. I'm timing you. If we're not in the elevator in fifteen, you owe me a pizza."

"Deal. No stalling, though." One corner of Jack's mouth went up.

"Me, stall? I'm the one who doesn't want to make this stop."

Jack glanced at his watch and raised his eyebrows. "Time hack." He knocked on Mara's door, which was a shiny stainless steel, a shade brighter than the ashy tint of the walls.

Zoe was surprised when Nico opened the door to the apartment, and she saw it wasn't impersonal and cold like the exterior, but had a modern design with warm hardwood floors and bursts of color in the red pillows on the boxy white furniture. The walls were covered with photos of Rome's fountains as well as modern paintings with splashes of primary colors.

Nico greeted them enthusiastically as if he hadn't just seen them a few days ago. He looked more mature than he had when they first met him. He still wore a causal fitted polo shirt and jeans like many young Italians she'd seen on the street, but he'd lost the skinny lankiness of adolescence. His face was wider now, and he'd filled out through the shoulders. He looked broader, more solid. He clasped Jack's hand, then turned to Zoe and kissed her warmly on both cheeks. He stepped back, catching her hand and pulling it to his chest, drawing them into the apartment. "You look as beautiful as ever."

"And you're as full of it as ever."

He tilted his head down and looked at her with sad dark-fringed eyes. "You do not know how your cruel words wound me."

Zoe pulled her hand away and patted his shoulder. "You'll get over it. You always do."

A grin split his face, and he shrugged. "I must go on."

"You know, you'll have to give up this flirting when you're married." Zoe glanced at a framed photo of the couple. They'd met Mara when they had dinner, and there had been just the slightest hint of hostility from Mara toward Zoe. Mara had masses of dark brown hair, a severe Roman nose, and a commanding manner, which Nico didn't seem to mind. "I don't think Mara will like it."

"Ah, but that is what Mara is doing, reforming me. A woman like Mara, she needs a project." He tapped his chest. "I will keep her busy for years."

Jack shook his head. "Be careful, Nico. It's impossible to completely understand a woman." Jack shot a look at Zoe as he said, "They're more complex than a physics equation."

Zoe said, "He's learned just how much he doesn't know about me. He's catching on."

Nico laughed. "You two, always with the joking. Come in, come in." He waved them toward the couch in the living area, apologized that Mara wasn't there, explaining she was away for a work-related conference in Florence. He offered them something to drink then brought them three bottles of mineral water on a tray with glasses. He poured the water, handed the glasses out, and then took a seat in a black club chair. He sipped from his glass, and his face turned somber. "Now, this is a serious problem, my friend." He gestured at a laptop computer on the coffee table, which sat alongside a phone and a stack of papers. "The theft."

Zoe couldn't quite see the screen, so she said, "It's in the news?"

Nico swiveled the laptop toward her. Above a close-up of the Flawless Set, the English headline proclaimed that world famous jewels had been stolen while they were on loan in Rome. "The incident reflects poorly on Italy, or so the article states. Italian officials are determined to..." he waved his hands around as he searched for the idiom he wanted—he'd always been a big fan of idioms, Zoe remembered. "...nip it in the bud," he finished. "They do not want to be tainted with the reputation as a place where the wealthy—and their jewels—are not safe."

"That explains why Alessi is pressing so hard," Jack said. "I thought there was a lot of manpower on the case."

Zoe frowned. "Nothing motivates like bad publicity."

"We had nothing to do with it," Jack said.

Nico said, "I did not think you did, even for a minute. No, this is another instance of bad timing, I think."

"More like bad associates," Jack said.

Nico picked up a magazine, which was folded open to an interior page. He handed it to Jack. "Take a look at that. Let me get you some more water," he said to Zoe.

Zoe had drained her glass. "Oh, that's fine."

Nico glanced pointedly at the magazine, then stood and took her glass from her hand. "No, I insist." He left the room for the kitchen.

"What was all that about?" Zoe asked Jack, but he just waved her closer and nodded at the magazine.

"He's trying to tell us, this is the guy we want." Jack pointed to a circled photograph.

"Christopher McKinley? But you asked him who Harrington would try to sell the Flawless Set to, right? It can't be McKinley. He's a celebrity reporter." Zoe had seen the half-hour cable entertainment show he hosted.

The article was a montage of photos of men under the headline that Zoe could only decipher a few words of because it was in Italian. "What is the headline?"

"World's Sexiest Bachelors," Jack said. McKinley stood barefoot on a palm-tree lined beach with the cuffs of his tuxedo pants rolled up to his calves and the buttons on his shirt open to the waist. His fair hair was clipped short and a dusting of stubble covered his jaw. He held a bottle of Champagne in one hand and two long-stemmed glasses in the other and had a rough-and-tumble vibe that came through in the photograph. Jack read the caption, " 'British television presenter, McKinley, 37, is known for his killer smile and cajoling the world's rich and famous into revealing intimate details.' "

"A gossip show host? No, it can't be him."

"Why not? Sounds like a good cover to me," Jack said. "No one would take him seriously. He is on the road a lot for his job, which lets him mingle with the extremely rich. Sounds ideal, in fact."

"So Christopher McKinley is some sort of fence to the rich and famous?" Zoe said, trying out the idea. It was hard to wrap her mind around the concept. Recently, McKinley's name had popped up in the grocery store tabloids as part of a love triangle that caused the break-up of a celebrity marriage, if you believed the articles. After her run-ins with the media, Zoe took all news items with more than a grain of salt, but was he a criminal as well as a cad? "It's just hard to imagine..."

She broke off as Nico returned with a fresh glass of fizzy water for her.

He sat down. "Yes, it is hard to imagine, but I assure you, he is the man you want to find."

"But isn't he in England?" Zoe asked. "Are you saying there are no jewelry fences here in Rome that Harrington could take the Flawless to?"

"Well, of course there are fences here," Nico said with a slightly offended air as if she'd insulted him by doubting Rome's possible black market network. "If the theft of the Flawless Set had been a typical smash and grab, then yes, your man would probably have gone to someone here locally, but the way the Flawless Set was stolen was different—there was elaborate planning, no? And the set itself, some of the value is in the history, the story, behind it."

Nico settled back in his chair. "In most cases, a thief would make more by breaking up the set and recutting the stones—and I am sure that is still an option with the Flawless because the stones themselves are spectacular—but if it could be sold intact, the mystique of it alone, adds value, keeping the price high. But to sell a piece like the Flawless necklace intact," he shrugged, "you would need someone with the right connections." Nico looked pointedly at the magazine.

"And McKinley is that person?"

"Sì. First, he is a countryman of Harrington's, is he not?"

"Yes, but that doesn't necessarily mean he would use him."

"No, but it is a connection. A slight one, I'll grant you, but it is still there. Of more importance is the fact that the word is out—at least among my associates—that if you need extremely high value jewels stolen, McKinley is your man."

"When you *need* something stolen? I don't understand."

"So that you can collect the insurance money."

"Oh, I see." Zoe sat back, trying to comprehend the idea that someone would plan a robbery to claim insurance money.

"It is a specialized market segment he caters to," Nico explained. "At a certain point the expenditure of insuring certain pieces is so high that it becomes, well, cost prohibitive. Often the value of the jewels does not increase enough to cover the price of insuring them over time." Nico shrugged. "That is where McKinley has found a niche. He arranges for the 'theft,' and after the insurance pays, McKinley gets his cut. The piece is either quietly returned, or—and this is more often the case—he delivers it to a cutter where it seamlessly reenters the market after it is recut and a certificate is forged to show it came from some other location. Of course, pieces like the Flawless Set, McKinley will do all he can to sell it intact to the right—elite—buyer." Nico finished his water and set down his glass with a click. "There is a second reason to find McKinley. I asked around and a dignified older man with a British accent was looking to meet McKinley."

"You've been a big help." Jack checked the time as he handed the magazine back to Nico, who tossed it into a basket near the couch with more glossy covers. "Mara likes to keep up with the celebrity news." He glanced at the cover then back at Jack. "In fact, Mara was telling me the other day that McKinley will be in Ischgl on Monday for a charity ski race event."

Zoe had been checking her watch, but looked up. "Ischgl. That doesn't sound like it's in England."

"No. Austria."

"It wouldn't happen to be anywhere near Lermoos would it?"

"I don't know, but Austria is not a big country." Nico pulled the laptop closer and typed. "Yes, they are both in Austria. About eighty kilometers apart."

Zoe looked at Jack. She didn't have to say anything. The travel printouts showed Harrington needed directions to Austria. McKinley was scheduled to be in Austria at that same time...

Jack stood and held out his hand to Nico. "Thank you."

"Stay for another drink? A coffee?"

"That would be—" Zoe began.

"No, we really must go." Jack said, shooting a sideways glance at Zoe.

One minute, she mouthed back at him.

Nico again tried to convince them to stay, but Jack hustled them to the door. "I'll walk out with you then. I have a meeting," Nico said, and they had to wait by the door as Nico gathered up his keys and his phone.

"I'll hold the elevator," Jack called and opened the door.

Zoe followed him into the hallway where he was repeatedly punching the DOWN button. The elevator arrived with a ding, the doors glided open, and they stepped in, both of them checking their watches.

"Twenty seconds over." Jack grimaced. "I'm losing my touch."

"I'm in the mood for Margherita pizza, I think."

"We'll look for something on the way to Austria."

Zoe nodded. They didn't need to discuss it. They had to go. It was the only lead they had. The only question was how they would travel. "Even though a flight is the quickest way, that might not be the best way for us to travel."

Jack kept his finger pressed on the button to keep the doors open as he replied. "Leaves too much of a trail. We'd have to use a credit card," Jack agreed. "And the train would be the same, unless we paid in cash, and we don't have enough to buy two tickets from here to Austria, anyway. No, we need something more under the radar."

"Like a car," Zoe said as Nico joined them in the elevator, apologizing for the delay. "Except we have the same credit card issue with renting a car," Zoe said. "I suppose we could try to buy one... but how would we pay for it? Our daily cash withdrawal limit is too low to get enough money, even for a clunker."

Nico said, "You need a car? Borrow one."

Jack pressed the button for the lobby. "Can't take a chance on something like that."

Nico looked offended. "I don't operate that way. Well, not anymore." He smiled faintly. "I am not a kid in Napoli. No, I mean use a car and return it."

"We can't take yours," Jack said. "That would link us too closely to you. You've already taken a chance by talking to us. We don't want to do anything else—"

Nico cut him off. "Not my car. Mara's. She won't mind. Come, I'll show you."

A few minutes later, they stood in a parking garage not far from the apartment in front of a sunflower yellow Fiat while Nico worked a key off his key ring. "It is perfect. Small, easy to drive. Good gas mileage. It is a little bright, yes, but there is no paperwork."

Jack reached for the key and thanked Nico. She could tell Jack would have rather have had another option, but short of stealing a car, this was their best choice. They said good-bye to Nico, and climbed in the car.

"I have to say I'm surprised," Zoe said.

"That I took Nico up on his offer? It's not exactly nondescript,

I'll give you that," Jack said as he started it, "but we have to work with what we've got."

"No, that Mara has such a...cheerful car. Yellow. Maybe she and Nico will work out after all."

10

"I DON'T THINK ALESSI WILL be happy that we left Rome." Zoe kept her gaze on the twin beams of the Fiat's headlights, which cut through the darkness, illuminating the strip of road and an occasional road sign. For the moment, they were alone on the road as they drove north, their lights the only specks of brightness in the night except for the pinpoints of the stars overhead. Streetlights were few and far between on the rural portions of the Autostrada.

A quick check of a road map that they bought on their way out of Rome confirmed that Nico was right. Both Ischgl and Lermoos were in Austria, a little over an hour and a half apart. They had swept along the road, passing turnoffs for city after city, Florence, Bologna, Milan, each just a name on a sign, and Zoe felt only a faint twist of longing as they gained on, then passed each destination. Their situation had her wanderlust firmly in check.

"No, Alessi wouldn't like it. Although, he never actually told us not to leave." Using his cell phone as a flashlight, Jack checked the map, creating a reflection of his profile on the passenger window against the opaque blackness.

"I think he'd consider it one of those things that are implied," Zoe said. "Something that didn't have to be stated."

"I'm sure he would. Hopefully, he won't realize we've left the city at all."

They had made a quick detour to their hotel before they left Rome. After parking the car in a nearby garage, they returned to their room long enough to pick up a change of clothes and a few other essentials, such as Jack's backpack. Jack had said they shouldn't bring their suitcase, and Zoe agreed. Neither of them had spotted the man or woman who'd been trailing them earlier, but the shift could have changed. They might have new watchers, people they didn't recognize. Neither Jack nor Zoe wanted to tip off anyone that they were leaving Rome—even if it was just for a few days. Their hotel was paid through the next week, which gave them a full three days to salvage their reputations.

Zoe had stuffed the essentials—a change of clothing and toiletries into her messenger bag while Jack had done the same, filling his backpack. They had turned in their key and mentioned dinner plans as well as discussed a possible tour of Tivoli as well as Ostia, two popular day trip destinations, with the afternoon desk clerk. If Alessi did notice they were gone, they hoped he would assume they'd gone on one of the excursions, buying them some time.

She moved her hands on the wheel, gripping it tightly. "Somehow, I think that's too much to hope for."

"Don't think about Alessi. Even if he realized we're gone, he won't be able to figure out where we are. He can't trace our cell phone. We didn't rent a car or take a flight out of Rome. We have enough cash that we can buy gas without using a credit card."

They'd stopped at an ATM before they left the city and made a large withdrawal, but they'd been doing that every few days, using the money to pay for food and entrance fees, so that transaction wouldn't raise any flags. "Even if he does find out we've left, we're okay," Jack continued. "We'll find Harrington then follow him. Hopefully, he'll meet McKinley in Ischgl to sell the jewels. We can alert Alessi, and the police can scoop them both up—the thief and the fence. If he can make two arrests and recover the jewels, he won't complain, and we'll be in the clear of the theft of the Flawless Set, which will clear us of the other robberies because there's nothing to link us to them except speculation."

"The part about alerting Alessi is a bit vague," Zoe said. "How are we going to do that? And how will Alessi be able to swoop in and make arrests in another country?"

"You've obviously never seen Interpol at work. I have. Believe me, these European countries can cooperate with frightening efficiency. Frightening, for criminals, that is. I can't believe that either Italy nor Austria will be willing to let a jewel thief walk away with the Flawless Set. Any police force would love to have the good PR associated with recovering such a famous set of jewelry."

Zoe shifted her hands on the wheel again. "I know. It's a good plan. Well, it's a plan. It's as good a plan as we're going to get. It's this all-encompassing blackness. Makes me edgy. And don't you dare make any comments about being afraid of the dark."

"Wouldn't dream of it. We all have something that sets the butterflies flapping. For me, I'd rather eat glass than do anything that puts me anywhere above ten feet off the ground. For you, it's hospitals—"

"You remembered that, did you?"

"Of course. You're rarely scared of anything, so I'm not about to forget one of the few times I've seen you looking absolutely terrified."

"Not *absolutely* terrified."

"Oh, absolutely. It was definitely, absolutely terrified. You looked like I would if I'd found out I had to walk across the Grand

Canyon on a wire. Absolutely terrified. But back to the darkness. Think of it this way—darkness is good."

"How?"

"It makes it easy to be sure we're alone." Jack glanced out the rear window. "No tail. Just pitch black, as far as the eye can see."

"I still don't like it."

"Want me to take over?"

"No, you should get some more sleep." Jack had driven for several hours while Zoe slept fitfully in the passenger seat. Now it was his turn. "I'll just concentrate on how tiny and isolated and safe the absolute pitch blackness makes me feel. I'll wake you in a few hours."

"Okay. Brenner Pass is coming up then we'll be in Austria. Not far to go."

They switched places again after a stop for a quick breakfast at a McDonald's with a view of the Alps so stunning that it could have been a five-star restaurant. It was early, only a little after six in the morning, but the horizon had begun to lighten around five, and now the rough peaks of the mountains were washed with the pink of sunrise. Zoe thought the growing brightness would make it harder for her to sleep, but she dropped off quickly and awoke later with a crick in her neck. She sat up and stretched.

"Oh good. You're awake. You can navigate." Jack handed her a coffee cup and the papers with the driving directions.

Zoe gratefully sipped the steaming coffee. "When did you get this?"

"Stopped about ten minutes ago. You slept right through. Didn't have the heart to wake you."

Zoe sipped some more, blinked, and wrapped both hands

around the warm cup. The temperature had been dropping the farther north they drove, and now it was actually cold. Jack had switched on the heater, and Zoe was glad she'd changed into her one pair of jeans she'd brought. Jack knew her well enough to leave her alone until the caffeine worked its way to her groggy brain. After a few minutes, Zoe looked at the driving directions, then the map. "Where are we?"

"Ah, I knew you'd come back to the land of the living if I gave you coffee."

"You are disgustingly cheery in the morning."

"Good thing you love me anyway."

"Good thing. Otherwise, I might murder you."

"Right. Disregarding that comment. We're through Innsbruck and off the main highway. We should be in Lermoos soon. You can read off the directions from there."

Zoe took another gulp of her coffee. "Sure."

Since they didn't have the address of the final destination listed on the papers she'd retrieved from Harrington's trashcan, they'd decided to drive to Lermoos and follow the driving directions.

"I hope he has the diamonds with him," Zoe said.

"So we're continuing with the dreary disposition?"

"Jack, you have to have thought about it, too. What if we've come all this way, and he ditched them before he got here? He could have stopped anywhere along that stretch of dark road and dropped them off with someone or hidden them."

"Then why would he go to Austria?" Jack asked. "Why leave Rome? Why ask around about McKinley? Why drive all this way?"

"Maybe he likes to ski."

Jack frowned. "I see him as more of a fly-fishing type of guy."

"Be serious. What are we going to do if he doesn't have the diamonds? Or, what if we're completely wrong, and he's not even here?"

"You're usually not so negative."

"I'm not usually a suspect in a jewel heist either," Zoe snapped then ran her hand over her face. "Sorry. I should have a rule. No conversation until my second cup of coffee."

"It's okay. I'm worried, as well, but before we get too carried away, let's see exactly what our situation is."

The road dropped down through densely forested hills that were layered with snow into an alpine village on the edge of a wide valley dotted with small wooden sheds. Snow piled along the side of the road and stood several inches deep on the roofs of white stucco houses with wooden balconies, but the roads and sidewalks were clear. Murals decorated the stucco of some of the buildings, ranging from religious scenes to ornate lettering with hotel names. On the other side of the valley, wisps of clouds shifted and snagged on the craggy, snow-covered mountain that dominated the valley. Around the foothills of the valley, ski gondolas dangled, motionless in the quiet morning air on a network of lift cables that climbed through the lower slopes to the mountains along white swaths where trees had been cleared.

They maneuvered through the little village, passing a church with a curved onion-dome bell tower, and Zoe directed Jack to a road that hugged the valley and took them closer to the towering mountain, but before they reached the foothills, they came to their next turn.

"It says take a left, here," Zoe said, catching a glimpse of a sign as Jack turned under a bridge and they plunged back into the forest. "I know where we are. That was a sign for the Zugspitze. I remember it from one of the guidebooks I copyedited. It's the highest mountain in Germany, but it actually straddles the Germany-Austria border."

"And we've just entered Germany." Jack nodded at a sign. The road twisted through a narrow valley, skirted around the

Zugspitze, and followed the sweeping course of a tumbling river with ice-edged banks. Unlike the wide, populated valley they'd just traveled through, this area was more rural with only a few buildings scattered far apart.

"The directions say we keep straight for another ten kilometers or so."

They passed a few signs for smaller towns and recreation areas and then they swept into Garmisch-Partenkirchen. Unlike the small villages on the other side of the mountain, Garmisch was a good-sized town. It was early, and the main street was quiet as they cruised by large neighborhoods of alpine-style homes, clothing shops, and restaurants. Only the bakeries were open, and Zoe's mouth watered at the thought of fresh baked bread, but she didn't suggest they stop.

Instead, she read off more directions. "At the Marienplatz, turn right. The hotel is on your right."

Jack made the turn and slipped into an open slot in a small parking lot between a hotel and a pedestrian zone that ran alongside another church with a rounded onion-shaped dome.

"That must be it," Zoe said, looking toward a hotel with carved wooden balconies running along each of its two stories and mosaic curlicues painted over each window. The name, Hotel Bavaria Alpina, was painted in gothic script on the side of the building above a mural of the mountain range.

Jack turned off the ignition. "It's early, hopefully he hasn't left his room yet."

"It doesn't look like anyone's left their room yet."

They watched the hotel for a few minutes, but even in that short amount of time, the temperature inside the car dropped quickly. Zoe's gaze shifted from the quiet hotel to the street in front of them where a few people had appeared. Some were walking dogs, others held baskets and appeared to be setting out to do their shopping. She looked back to the hotel. "I wish there was some way to know for sure if he's checked in." Zoe blew on her hands. "How cold do you think it is here?" She pulled her light-weight cardigan tighter. It was the only long-sleeved thing she'd brought. She'd thrown it in her suitcase in Dallas, thinking that she could wear it on the plane when they were at altitude. Even with a thin shirt layered under it, the combination was no match for the Alps. Her feet, bare inside her skimpy leather sandals, which had been perfect for the warm Roman weather, were icy already.

"Probably around freezing now." He glanced up at the sky. "Since it's a clear day, it should warm up. Maybe it will get up into the forties."

"Let's hope it does because we are not dressed for this weather."

They sat for an hour, watching as the Hotel Bavaria Alpina came to life and the sun climbed higher in the sky, but even when the sunlight crept across the windshield, the car didn't warm up, and Jack intermittently started the engine so they could run the heater for a few minutes. Some guests departed the hotel, dragging suitcases to cars or taxis, and traffic gradually picked up on the main road.

Zoe wiggled in her seat. "Good grief, this is boring. If we don't see Harrington soon, you're going to have to restrain me from going in there. You know they have heat. And food. Probably a breakfast buffet with soft warm rolls and steaming coffee and—"

Jack sat up straight. "I think that's Harrington."

11

D RESSED IN A TRENCH COAT, wool scarf, and leather gloves, Harrington trotted down the steps of the hotel and came toward them. Zoe and Jack both ducked, but Harrington continued by them to the pedestrian area.

Jack opened his door. "Let's go."

Zoe hopped out, glad to be moving, but as cold as it was inside the car, it was colder outside. The frigid temperature quickly penetrated the lightweight shirt and cardigan. At least she had on jeans. The pedestrian area wasn't crowded so it wasn't hard to keep Harrington in sight, but that also meant they had to stay back at least half a block.

They trailed him along the cobblestoned street, passing beer gardens shut up against the morning sun and clothing stores just opening for the day. Harrington crossed the street and went into a bakery. He ordered at the counter, then sat near the window, sipping his coffee and eating a pastry.

"Coffee. I am so jealous," Zoe said, watching from across the street as she shifted from one foot to the other. "Even if we're only going to be here a day, we have to get some more clothes," Zoe said, scanning the street. "My fingernails are turning a pale blue, and we're drawing attention." A passerby wearing a wool coat gave them a long, curious look. "There's a boutique a few doors down. I'll see if they have anything we can afford," Zoe said.

"Good idea. I'll stay on Harrington. Looks like there is another bakery at that end of the street. Why don't you get us some more coffee and something to eat?"

"Already part of my plan." Zoe scurried away.

Zoe pushed into the boutique and relished the toasty warmth. She went directly to a rack of winter coats and nearly passed out when she checked the price tags. As she browsed the rest of the store, she did some quick mental math, totaling up what they'd spent on gas and tolls on the way north and mentally subtracted that amount from the total cash they'd brought with them because they'd need at least that amount to get back to Rome. There was no way she and Jack were restocking their wardrobe, at least not at this store. She bought coffee and two pastries, and caught up with Jack as he came out of the bakery where Harrington had been.

She handed Jack his coffee as he scanned the street. "There he is, not too far ahead of us. Looks like he's going back to the hotel."

Now that she had a free hand, Zoe delved into the bag and brought out the pastries, glazed swirls of berries and poppy seeds nestled inside a donut-like bread. They ate as they walked, shadowing Harrington from several yards away.

"He didn't meet anyone?"

"No. Before he left, he went back to the counter, unfolded a map, and asked some questions. I went in after he left, and said the white-haired man had left a cell phone on the table, and did they know where he went?"

"Smart."

Jack ate the last two bites of the pastry and sighed. "You can always count on the Germans to throw everything they can into a pastry." He crumpled the bag. "They said he asked directions to the Zugspitze cable car and its opening time."

"He's going to the top of the mountain?" She looked at the highest peak in the distance.

"Afraid so."

"We're going to freeze to death"

"No joy on the winter clothes?"

Zoe licked the last of the glaze from her fingers. "Only if we can both fit into one coat, and even then, the price is outrageous."

"It is a boutique in a mountain resort town."

"I know. Like I said, we're going to get frostbite, especially if we're going to the peak. You know it will be colder up there."

"True, but Harrington also asked about places to have lunch on the mountain, so we may have a few hours before he heads out. We may be able to find something cheaper."

"I don't know. Like you said, resort town. If this were a movie, there would be a street fair or street vendors, and we could just shoplift warmer clothes. Or someone would conveniently leave their coat on the back of their chair, and we could walk by quickly and take it with no one noticing."

"Yeah, well. We'd need *two* coats, and I don't think even one person will be leaving their coat lying around unattended in zero-degree weather," Jack said.

They cautiously turned the corner at the edge of the pedestrian zone and checked the Hotel Bavaria Alpina. Harrington strolled up the steps and disappeared inside. Zoe tossed their trash and glanced around. "Okay, ready for some hit and run shopping?"

"Let's ask a question or two first. You keep an eye on the hotel." Jack disappeared into an apotheke. He emerged from the drug store within seconds, a smile on his face. "There's a second-hand clothing and sports equipment resale shop two blocks over."

"You're a genius."

"Glad you think so. See what you can find. I'll stay on the hotel." He told her where the shop was located. "Be fast. And no lederhosen for me," he called after her.

"No promises. You'll have to take whatever is in stock," she tossed over her shoulder as she jogged up the street and around the corner.

She found the second hand shop easily and was relieved when she checked a few price tags. The racks were stuffed with everything from high-end designer clothes to casual everyday clothes. One section was filled with used ski clothes and another held an assortment of the traditional Bavarian costumes for men and women. Zoe passed the traditional dress with a smile, thinking of Jack's reaction if she brought him the embroidered leather shorts that Bavarians wore with knee socks. Zoe quickly found an insulated ski jacket in powder blue for herself and picked a men's jacket in gray for Jack. Then she added two pairs of thick wool socks as well as a pair of snow boots with a red slash through the price tag. Thank goodness Jack had brought a pair of leather driving shoes, so she only needed one pair of shoes.

Now, they just needed hats and gloves, and they'd be set. The only gloves in the shop were insulated waterproof ski gloves, and the price made Zoe's eyebrows shoot up. Living in Dallas, she didn't have much need for gloves so she didn't know their typical price range, but fifty euro and up was beyond her budget. They'd just have to keep their hands in their pockets. She quickly sorted through the knit ski hats and picked the two most understated, which wasn't saying much. One was a key pattern in green, yellow, and pink and the other was a black and white snowflake pattern with braided tassels dangling from earflaps.

She put everything on the counter in front of a happy sales clerk, a young woman wearing a dirndl, the traditional Bavarian costume for women with the full skirt covered with an apron, a laced bodice, and a white shirt with puffy sleeves.

Zoe had enough money for everything but the hats. She reached to put them back, but the sales girl smiled and said something in rapid German that Zoe couldn't begin to decipher. The girl put the hats firmly in the bag and handed it to Zoe with the receipt.

"Vielen dank," Zoe said, meaning each word deeply and hurried out of the shop. Jack had the car running. He must have been watching for her because as soon as she came into sight, he pulled out of the parking lot and stopped the car by her on the sidewalk.

She slid into the car and slammed the door. "Jackpot."

"Perfect timing. Harrington just left. He's about a block ahead of us in that white Jetta."

"Do you think he's going to the Zugspitze?"

"Maybe. If he stays on this road, he could be." They were cruising through the town, backtracking on the same road they'd arrived on.

"Well, if he does go to the peak, we're prepared." She handed the knit hat with the tassels to Jack. He shot her an incredulous look.

"Hey, it's warm, and you've got the understated one." Zoe pulled out the bright, multicolored hat and ripped off the price tag before working it down over her ears.

"Well, at least yours matches the car," Jack said.

Zoe rolled her eyes. "You should be glad. I could have brought you leather shorts and one of those fedora-like Bavarian hats with a feather. I didn't think you'd want that."

Jack grinned. "Only if you're wearing a dirndl."

"Not likely, at least at these temperatures. Bavarians are hearty

—shorts for the men and dresses with low necklines for the women and no boots. Oh, he's signaling."

They followed the car, making the turn onto a road that wound through several villages. Jack hung back, barely keeping the white car in sight. Zoe spent the drive working her feet into the wool socks and boots. Then she removed the tags from both jackets and shrugged into hers just as they followed the white car into a parking lot for the cable car lift. "Guess we are going up." Jack parked a few rows away from the Jetta. He donned his hat and jacket as they shadowed Harrington, who bought a ticket for the cable car.

They lingered until Harrington moved away then purchased their own tickets and went to wait on the platform for the cable car with several people between themselves and Harrington. "Maybe we should wait for the next cable car," Zoe said in an undertone.

"No. We can't risk losing him." Jack tapped the brochure's map that they'd been given with their tickets. "It's thirty minutes until the next cable car departs for the top. Once he's at the peak, there's a second cable car up there that he could take to another area. Looks like this car will be packed. Whatever side he goes on, we'll take the other. We should be okay as long as you keep your hair under that hat."

Zoe tucked a few strands of hair up into her hat. "I'll keep mine on if you keep yours on."

Jack glanced over his shoulder, which sent the tassels swishing. One got stuck in his collar, and he batted it away. "I'm buying a pocket knife up there and cutting these things off."

"I think you look cute."

Jack's eyes narrowed. "Next time, I shop and you watch."

The large cable car slid into place, and they crowded in, moving to the opposite side from Harrington. There had to be at least thirty-five or forty people in the car. Within seconds, the spacious car was packed with people riding up for the view as well as people wearing helmets and carrying skis, poles, and snowboards. "At least it's so packed we don't have to worry about Harrington drifting from the front to the back."

"No, there's no way anyone could even move a step."

The doors closed, the car shifted, paused, and then swept away from the platform, and Zoe forgot all about keeping an eye on Harrington. The view was incredible. As they moved up the mountain, a lake rimmed in snow-dusted pine trees came into sight in the distance, its vivid blue water sparkling in the sunlight. Directly below them, evergreen trees, their branches heavy with snow, marched up the side of the mountain. The car swayed and rocked as they passed one of the support towers. Gradually, the trees thinned and the mountains on the horizon dominated the view. Jagged peaks covered in snow spread out as far as they could see.

Jack slipped his arm around Zoe's waist, and she leaned into him. "Not quite what I expected to see on my Italian vacation, but I love it."

He dropped a kiss on her lips, and then they looked back at the view. The cables were now running almost completely vertical, pulling them up a sheer rock face layered in snow. No trees, no bushes, no hint of vegetation, broke the white of the snow or the pale gray of the rock. They rocked over another support, this one caked in snow and ice. Zoe swallowed and her ears popped as they went up and up, the other snow-capped mountains dropping away below them. It was a clear day, but Zoe remembered from her guidebook editing that the weather at the top of the mountain was fickle and could change quickly. A layer of clouds hovered in the distance on one side of the mountain, and Zoe wondered if the clouds were moving toward them or away from them.

The car slid into the arrival platform. "That was too short," Zoe said.

"Nothing like climbing six thousand feet in ten minutes, is there?"

"I want to do it again."

"Good thing it's a round trip deal then." They hung back, letting other people depart first and stepped off after Harrington. They followed him to the observation deck at the top of the building, which was a spacious open-air platform that stretched across the border between Germany and Austria with a beer garden, a souvenir stall, and a stand selling snacks and beer. Rows of picnic tables were filled with people eating, smoking, and sipping huge mugs of beer. A strong wind cut through the thick layers of their clothes. Zoe burrowed her hands deeper into her pockets and surveyed the view. She nodded to the other side of the platform. "See the sign for Tyrol? That's Austria. Before the EU, you could walk across and get your passport stamped."

Harrington strolled, admiring the amazing view, and Zoe was a little disappointed he didn't cross over to Austria, but instead stayed on the German side. They trailed along behind him. The bank of clouds she'd seen on the way up was closing in, but for the moment, the view was clear. The peaks of mountains spread out below them in the distance while up close the area around the viewing platform—the peak of the mountain—was stark and barren. Where patches of snow had been cleared, the ground was pale and rocky. They paused by one of the telescopes as Zoe said, "On one hand, it's so bleak and inhospitable looking that it makes me think of a moonscape."

"Or some post-apocalyptic movie set."

"But it's beautiful, too. The sky looks so blue against the rock and the wisps of clouds...can you believe they're trailing along below us? Oh, look, climbers." Zoe pointed to a tiny trail of specks moving up the side of the mountain. "They're so far way they look like ants."

"Just reminds you what an immense setting this is. Time to move on." He nodded to the snack stand where Harrington stood in line. He bought a sausage and took a seat at one of the picnic tables lined up on the platform.

"Looks like we're eating outside," Zoe said. "I was never so glad to own a coat."

They ordered sausages and pretzels and moved to a table directly behind Harrington. Zoe sat down back to back with Harrington. Keeping her voice low as she pulled off a piece of the pretzel, which was soft and warm, she asked, "Anything?"

Jack chewed a bite of the spicy sausage and shook his head, which sent the tassels waving. He swallowed. "Nothing. Just eating."

"Well, I'm glad we get to eat. It's not the pizza—which you still owe me. I haven't forgotten—but it's delicious."

"Wait, a man sat down across from Harrington."

12

GEMMA STILL COULDN'T QUITE BELIEVE the files they'd found yesterday in the apartment that Harrington Throckmorton had rented. It was all there—every detail about the country house robberies. Who would have thought that she'd find it in Rome of all places? But, she supposed, if you were a jewel thief and the amazing Flawless Set was on display for the first time in years, then Rome was the place to be. Strange that there was no file on the Flawless Set, though.

And what was odder still was that she didn't remember any mention of this Harrington Throckmorton or the Andrews couple in connection with the country house thefts. She was scrolling through her notes on her phone, looking for any link between the three people and the country house thefts when a young lieutenant hurried into Alessi's office and did a double take when his gaze fell on Gemma. She had taken up residence at a table in the corner. A forensics team was working at the apartment today, but she was sticking close to Alessi, who had returned to the office. Every bit of news and information about the case would come to him, and she didn't want to miss anything.

The lieutenant slowed down enough to give her a lingering smile. Alessi snapped out a final instruction into the phone. Gemma couldn't help overhearing. The one-sided conversation was in Italian, but she picked up enough words to figure out he was working on another case, something involving stolen statues. Alessi dropped the phone into the cradle, which pulled the young man's attention away from Gemma.

Alessi and the man had a short exchange in Italian then the young man left with one last smile at Gemma.

"A new charge on Harrington Throckmorton's credit card," Alessi said with a sigh. "A ticket for the Zugspitze."

Gemma raised her eyebrows. "Germany."

"Why couldn't he have stayed in Italy?"

Alessi reached for the phone then called the young man back, who appeared so suddenly that he had to have been lingering outside the door. She caught the word "Andrews." After a few more questions, Alessi motioned the young man on his way and spun toward Gemma.

"There is no sign of the Andrews couple at their hotel. Desk clerk says they asked about Tivoli and Ostia last night. I'm having their room checked again as well as their credit cards and bank account."

"Maybe they're in Germany, too," Gemma said. Alessi frowned, clearly displeased at the thought they might have slipped out of his city. His desk phone rang and he reached for it. A long, conversation—an argument, really—in rapid-fire Italian followed. By the end of it, Alessi was standing, gesturing widely as he spoke. He finally slammed the phone down, muttering to himself.

He made another call, his attitude and voice slipping into resignation. Finally, he hung up. With his hand still on the phone, he looked at Gemma. "I am sorry, signorina, but I must leave. I will introduce you to my second-in-command before I go. He will keep you updated—"

"Where are you going?"

"To Germany." He said it as if he was leaving for Siberia. "My superiors insist. The theft of the Flawless Set is of primary importance. The news ...the embarrassment...the headlines. I must make every effort to recover it."

"I understand," Gemma said. She'd grabbed a newspaper and read it on the plane. The articles were not kind to the Italians, accusing them of lackluster security and shoddy investigation.

She understood the pressure, but there was no way she was staying in Rome if the investigation was moving to another country. "Good thing I travel light," Gemma said. "I'll meet you at the airport in an hour."

Zoe leaned to one side to give Jack a better view of the men seated at the picnic table behind her.

Jack pulled a napkin from under the anchor of the paper trays that held their sausages. The wind snagged it, and he reached over to pick it up before the wind whipped it over the edge of the platform. Jack straightened. "It's McKinley. Can you hear anything they're saying?"

Zoe tilted her head to the side and focused all her concentration on listening. After a few seconds, she shook her head. "Nothing. Either they're not talking, or they're speaking so quietly I can't hear them. Do you think...is he giving it to McKinley here?" If that was the case, things had moved too fast. They'd arrived too late to get Alessi involved before the Flawless Set changed hands. The horrible consequences of what that would mean settled on her like a heavy weight on her shoulders.

"Let's not panic yet. It looks like all they are doing is sitting."

Zoe reached for her messenger bag and pulled out the small camera she'd used to snap photos of all the tourist sights. "You know what we need? Pictures, so we'll have more than our word that they met."

"Good idea."

"Don't worry," she said before he could say anything else. "I'll use the zoom."

She ate another bite of her sausage, then inched her way out of the picnic bench seat, and went the long way around the building situated in the middle of the viewing platform, which housed the snack stand as well as stairs and elevators to the other levels of the building. She came out on the other side, snapped a few photos of the outcropping of rock topped by a golden cross that marked the highest point in Germany, then swiveled toward the rows of picnic tables.

She focused on the pair of men and hit the shutter several times. Through the viewfinder, she studied McKinley. He had a deep tan, curly golden hair, sparkling teeth, and wore a ski jacket, pants, and ski boots. A pair of waterproof gloves rested on the table by his pretzel.

He broke off a piece of pretzel and washed it down with a swallow of beer. He spoke a few words, and Harrington nodded then they continued to eat. Their lack of interaction made them look like they were simply two strangers who'd happened to sit down beside each other. The long rows of tables meant that different parties often sat beside each other, politely ignoring each other. But it couldn't be coincidence that the two men were seated across from each other, no matter how disinterested they seemed.

She meandered back around the far side of the building then took a few more pictures from the other angle to ensure that she had both of the men's faces clear in the pictures. As she watched,

McKinley crumpled his napkin and stood. Harrington rose as well. The men cleared their trash, and Zoe blinked. Something was wrong...different. She couldn't figure out what it was, but something had happened. Before she could pin it down, the men moved to the railing where they stood side by side.

Zoe looked at Jack. He motioned for her to stay where she was. Jack picked up their trash and dumped it in a trashcan that was close to the two men, then he went to a point farther along the railing and put his head down as if he were studying the panoramic map pinpointing all the peaks in view. The two men turned toward each other and shook hands. Zoe hit the shutter, trying to capture the image. Harrington strode away, and McKinley headed for the snack line again, which meant he was heading directly for Zoe. She faded to the right, moving to the railing where Jack met her.

They fell into step together as they followed Harrington back down to the cable car. Zoe glanced over her shoulder at McKinley. "Should we see what he does? Where he goes?"

"Looks like he's going for another beer. No, I think we'd better stay with Harrington. When I threw away the trash, I heard a few words. McKinley said, 'See you in Ischgl tomorrow' then Harrington nodded."

"They're meeting tomorrow so Harrington can sell him the Flawless Set." The rush of relief Zoe felt was so intense that she almost felt lightheaded for a moment.

"Well, they weren't that specific, and I only heard a few words, but yes, I think that's what they're planning. I did hear what I thought was the word wire transfer."

They hung back on the cable car platform as they waited in the line about ten people behind Harrington. Zoe had switched the camera to the review mode so she could look at the pictures she'd taken and was examining each one. The screen was tiny, so she zoomed in until the worn wood of the picnic table showed up in high definition so she could examine what the men had in front of them. Then she quickly skipped to the last photos, the one where the men were shaking hands.

"They did make a switch," Zoe said under her breath.

The car arrived, and they crowded on, again making sure to go to the opposite side of the car from Harrington. The atmosphere of this car was different from their last ride up. While the mood going up the mountain had been one of quiet expectation, on the way down their full car contained a large group of people in ski gear who obviously knew each other and had just come off the slopes. They loudly recounted their runs, laughing and joking, in a mix of English and German. Under the cover of their chatter, Jack and Zoe chatted quietly.

"What have you got?" Jack asked.

"They traded gloves." Zoe showed him the first photos of the men, their gloves resting on the table. "See, Harrington's brown leather gloves are beside his food, and McKinley's black waterproof ski gloves are beside his beer." She went to the last photo. "But here, where they are shaking hands, Harrington has the black waterproof gloves in his hand and McKinley is tucking the leather gloves into the pocket of his ski jacket. Neither one of them had gloves on when they parted."

"Interesting."

"Odd. I mean, I bet it's not even above zero at the top. I can see taking off your gloves to eat—maybe, but then why wouldn't you put them back on? I'd certainly wear gloves if I had any."

"You're right. They traded."

The short ride was over, and Zoe put the camera away as the car glided into the platform. She'd completely missed the scenery on the way down, but didn't even care. She was so consumed with thinking about the trade that a sick feeling descended on her.

"Jack, did we mess up? What if Harrington gave him the Flawless Set, right there in front of us? McKinley could have it now, and we're at the bottom of the mountain." There was another way down from the top, a cog railway, and there was another cable car that departed from the top of the Zugspitze that ferried skiers to the glacier and ski area slightly below the summit of the mountain. "Finding McKinley will be much harder. We don't know when he's coming down or what route he'll take. We might never find him."

They hung back again, waiting for Harrington to depart first. As he walked away through the rows of cars in the parking lot, Zoe glanced back at the cable car. "Maybe we should go back up—try to find McKinley."

"No, we've got to stay with Harrington. Bird in the hand and all that. They did exchange something, but I don't think McKinley has what we're looking for. Why arrange to meet tomorrow in Ischgl, if the deal was done today?" Jack headed for their yellow car, which seemed to glow among all the other understated blue, gray, and black cars that filled the lot.

"Unless it's to feed him more stuff from the other robberies," Zoe said as they got in the car. "Harrington told us that the other gems haven't been recovered. What if Harrington's been holding them?"

"Then why wouldn't he have done it now?" Jack countered as he pulled onto the road and followed the white Jetta from a good distance as it retraced its earlier route, heading back toward Garmisch.

"Because he wanted to get rid of the biggest piece, the most incriminating one first."

"Okay, that's possible. Here's another scenario," Jack said. "Harrington meets with McKinley today and McKinley gives Harrington a down payment on the Flawless Set to show he's serious. They meet tomorrow to complete the transaction. Or, Harrington was handing off the account info—McKinley needed the account number to set up everything for a wire transfer."

"I suppose that could have happened. And they'd want to meet in person instead of exchanging information like that over the phone or in an email."

"Right," Jack said. "Less traceable evidence if you avoid using phones and computers. And you have the added benefit that you actually see the guy face-to-face, get a feel for him."

Zoe sighed. "I hope it was just a preliminary meeting."

"Either way, they're meeting again tomorrow, so we're not sunk. We have to stay with Harrington, but make sure he doesn't know he's being followed." Jack's words slowed with the last sentence as he frowned at the road ahead. "Except that he *is* being followed."

"Did he spot us?"

"No, someone else is following him. See that gray hatchback? It's been on his tail since he left the cable car parking lot."

"Could be a coincidence, I suppose," Zoe said, thinking about the map. "There's only one road coming back from the cable car. The cars have to follow this same route."

They reached the main road, and Harrington's right blinker came on as he made the turn and headed toward Garmisch. The gray hatchback didn't pause or signal, just accelerated into the turn as if trying to keep as little space between the two cars as possible. "Not doing a good job of being inconspicuous, are they?" Zoe said.

"No, tailgating is generally frowned upon as a following technique."

"Maybe they've figured that out," Zoe said. "They're dropping back. No, wait—" she paused, then sucked in a breath. The driver of the gray hatchback must have floored it because the gray car closed in on Harrington's car in seconds. *There's going to be a wreck,* flashed through Zoe's mind, but before she could say the words, the driver of the gray hatchback veered slightly to the right, and instead of hitting the car directly in the back, the left front bumper of the gray car smashed into the rear bumper of Harrington's car. The force of the impact sent the white car off the road in an arc toward the thick line of trees that bordered the road. Red brake lights flared and tires churned snow as the car bumped through the rough surface toward the trees.

The gray hatchback's brake lights blazed, too. It straightened inside the lane lines then accelerated away down the dark strip of road. Harrington's car shot through the line of trees and disappeared into the thick darkness of the forest.

"Oh, look," Zoe said through fingers pressed to her lips.

Jack pulled to the side of the road, hit the hazard lights, and they were both out of the car and running toward the point where the tire tracks bisected the tree line.

13

I F THE TIRE TRACKS IN the snow hadn't made it obvious where the car had entered the trees, there was a spray of pine needles on the snow and a scrape across the trunk of one of the trees where the bark had been stripped away.

The band of trees that ran along the road was actually quite small, only stretching for a few yards to the bank of the wide, fast moving river that curved along the road. The white car rested on the embankment above a several foot drop down to the icy riverbank. The right headlight was planted in a tree trunk, and the hood of the small car was crumpled all the way to the windshield.

As they approached the car, there was no movement. They exchanged a glance as they slowed. Zoe knew Jack was thinking exactly what she was—that when Harrington saw them, everything changed. Their ability to shadow him and alert the police to the next meeting between Harrington and McKinley was gone. "We have to make sure he's okay," Zoe said.

"I know." Jack moved to the driver's side, which was dented. A long scrape ran along the entire length of the side. "The door is jammed." Harrington sat unmoving in the driver's seat and didn't react to their movements outside the car.

Zoe went around the other side and tried the passenger door. It opened easily. The airbag had deployed and a fine dust swirled through the air. Harrington looked okay except for a bloody nose and he seemed disoriented, a shocked look on his face. He slowly turned his head toward Zoe, stared at her for a long moment, then blinked and touched his nose. His fingers came away bloody, and he raised his eyebrows.

"You've been in an accident," Zoe said, searched the interior for something he could use to staunch the bleeding, but the car must have been a rental because it had that fresh new car smell, and there was absolutely nothing personal in the car, not even a crumpled napkin or gum wrapper.

Harrington looked around, taking in the trees and the river rushing loudly by them. "Hit and run, actually." Harrington tilted his head back and pinched the bridge of his nose.

"Yes. We saw the whole thing." Jack's tone was hard and unforgiving.

Zoe shot a look at Jack over the roof of the car. Harrington looked frail and shaky, not like someone who'd masterminded an elaborate jewel heist then pinned the blame on them.

"What are we going to do?" Zoe whispered as Jack came around to the open door.

"Play it by ear," Jack said, his attention drawn to the road, which they could see through the gaps in the trees. The traffic continued to move with an occasional vehicle sweeping by, but Jack was focused on a car that moved slower than normal.

"That's the gray hatchback," Zoe said. "Did they have an attack of conscience and come back to make sure everyone is okay?"

Harrington, sniffing and pressing his forearm to his nose,

clambered over the gearshift and into the passenger seat. He patted around on the floorboard and under the seats while he tried to keep his chin elevated. He made a satisfied grunting sound, pulled something from under the front seat, and crawled out of the car.

"Come on." He pushed between Zoe and Jack, gripped Zoe's arm, and towed her deeper into the trees. "Away from the car. We need to get away from the car. In case..." Jack followed them quickly and moved to disengage Harrington's grip, but Harrington dropped his hand, and his voice trailed off as the hatchback drew even with their yellow car.

Zoe squinted, but she couldn't distinguish anything about the driver in the hatchback, except the person seemed to be wearing a hat or hood. Maybe a hoodie? The engine revved, and the car accelerated away.

"That wasn't an attack of conscience." Jack looked at Harrington.

"More like a check of their handiwork." Harrington's words came out choppy as he paused to breathe deeply. He bent over and rested his hands on his knees as he caught his breath. "Sorry. Shock. And adrenaline, I suppose. Good thing you're here, or I wouldn't have stood a chance." Harrington straightened and pressed his sleeve once more to his nose experimentally, but it wasn't bleeding anymore. "Why are you here, by the way? No, never mind." He waved his own question away. "No time for that. Let me see if the car will start."

Jack gripped Harrington's arm, drawing him to a halt as Harrington tried to pass him.

"The only place you're going is with us, to talk to Alessi."

Harrington pulled back, confused, but Jack didn't let go. "Alessi?" Harrington asked. "I don't understand." His tone shifted from puzzled to affronted by the time he finished speaking, and he shot an offended glance at Jack's firm grip on his arm.

"Colonel Alessi of the Carabinieri. You're going to explain to him exactly how you framed us for the theft."

"Framed you—" He peered at Jack then looked to Zoe. She had her arms crossed. Harrington went as pale as the snow piled on the evergreen branches. "Theft?" He sagged, leaning against Jack. "There's been another one?"

"The Flawless Set." Jack's voice was dangerously quiet as he added, "But you already know that."

It didn't seem possible that Harrington could lose more color, but he did, his skin going a gray that made the blur of dried blood on his upper lip stand out even more. Harrington's gaze skipped from Jack to Zoe. He pulled himself together, straightened and carefully disengaged from Jack, who let him go, but Zoe could see that Jack was still on alert, ready to make a move if Harrington tried to run. Of course, she didn't think Harrington would have a chance against Jack in a foot race or any other type of physical contest. Apparently, Harrington had come to the same conclusion, because he chose talking over action. "And you're accusing me." His tone was formal, as if he was an attorney questioning a witness at trial.

"Yes. The Carabinieri are under the impression that we are responsible, but *we* know we didn't do it..."

Zoe stepped forward. "We saw you today. We know you met with McKinley, and we know about his reputation, his sideline business in stolen jewelry. We have photos of the exchange you made."

"Oh. And you think...ah, I see."

Harrington didn't say anything. Instead, he lifted his hand toward Zoe. Jack reacted, moving closer to her, but Harrington wasn't threatening her, only holding out his hand. The late afternoon sunlight was fading, and it was dim under the thick canopy of pine branches, so Zoe couldn't see what he held in his hand at first. As she took it from him, she felt the slippery surface of a waterproof fabric.

"It's *McKinley's* gloves. Well, only one," she amended. Something heavy, weighed it down. She tilted it over her palm and a cold, glittery mass of gold and sparkling stones landed in her hand.

It was the peacock brooch that had been stolen from Rowen House. It rested in her palm, the large opal glittering and sparkling with the faintest movement of her hand. The sapphires, emeralds, and diamonds interwoven among the gold winked in the light that filtered through the trees. "But this is..." Zoe looked in confusion from the stone to Harrington, her mind racing. "You exchanged gloves." She'd seen it with her own eyes. She had photos to prove it. "This was McKinley's glove. Why would he give you this brooch? Was he returning it?"

"In a way," Harrington said, watching her keenly with the same sort of encouraging, expectant gaze that her geometry teacher had fixed on her when he called on her in class.

"He couldn't fence it? Or is it a fake?" She looked again at the dazzling piece in her palm and immediately discarded that idea. Even to her untrained eye, she could see that the workmanship was beautiful, and the stones had a radiance that surely wasn't an imitation. Harrington said McKinley was *returning* the brooch... there was only one other possibility.

Zoe's gaze flew to Jack's face as she rearranged the bits and pieces of information they knew. It all made sense if you flipped everything around. It was like looking through a telescope the wrong way first—everything was distorted and fuzzy—but when you switched it around, the view was clear and sharp.

She could see Jack had the same thought. His face, even his stance, relaxed.

She looked back at Harrington. "You were *buying* it back, not selling."

He smiled as if she'd just correctly completed a geometry proof. "Yes. It was a recovery operation. The tip of the iceberg, I think."

"You mean McKinley has more?"

"He says he has the rest of them, and I certainly hope he wasn't lying, since I just handed him several thousand euros and promised him more tomorrow night. He said that there was more where that had come from."

Jack frowned. "Did he mean specifically from that robbery, or just more jewels in general?"

"Oh, he meant that robbery. He thinks I'm working in conjunction with the insurance company as an independent investigator so he knows I'm only interested in the Rowan House jewels."

"He knows you're connected with Millbank and Proust? And he's willing to talk to you?"

Harrington shrugged. "The police usually have little success with recovering stolen property, especially gems. A gem can be recut and entered into the legitimate retail market, making recovery extremely difficult—almost impossible. So insurance companies are often willing to ransom certain stolen items in order to get them back."

"But doesn't that just perpetuate the cycle?" Zoe asked.

"I didn't say it was a good system, or that I agreed with it. Millbank and Proust have an official policy of not paying ransom, but in this case—well, desperate times and all that. It seemed the only way. And, technically, Millbank and Proust aren't ransoming jewelry. I am, acting on my own."

That glimmer of concern she'd noticed during their meeting

before the exhibit hadn't shown the depth of his apprehension. He was so worried about his career that he was willing to operate outside normal boundaries, something Zoe couldn't fault him for. When your back was pressed against the wall, you sometimes had to do things outside normal channels.

"So if McKinley has this," Jack pointed to the brooch, "he could have the Flawless Set?"

"It's possible," Harrington said slowly. "But they've only been missing for what? A day? That's an awfully short amount of time. Logistics alone...getting them from Rome to here..."

"We came from Rome to here," Jack said. "No reason someone else couldn't do it."

"And all the Millbank and Proust employees were scurrying out of Rome as fast as possible," Zoe said.

"Like ancient Romans fleeing the barbarians," Jack said. "Some people had already left, right?"

"Yes. Carlo was gone, and Amy was on her way to the airport," Zoe said. "Mrs. Davray was scheduled to leave later that afternoon."

"Well, I'll definitely ask him tomorrow, let him know I'm interested in the Flawless Set as well."

Zoe ran her thumb over the smooth, icy cold stone. "Why the delay until tomorrow? Why not buy all the jewelry back now?"

"Two reasons. First, because McKinley is cautious." Harrington gestured to the brooch. "This little exchange was a test, for both of us. I proved I could produce the cash, and he proved he had the stolen goods."

Jack said, "Sort of a dry run for the larger deal?"

"Exactly."

"And the other reason?" Zoe asked.

"My retirement account has taken quite a hit. I can't afford to purchase the whole lot on my own."

Zoe blinked. "You bought this back with money from your retirement account?"

"I told you this whole operation is off-book. I don't know whom I can trust in Millbank and Proust. I couldn't afford to tip anyone off that I had a line on the stolen jewels."

Jack said, "If you're out of money, how are you planning to pay McKinley tomorrow?"

"Now that I have proof that McKinley has the jewels, I'd planned to directly contact the board of directors tonight to request a wire transfer to a Swiss bank account to buy the rest, which would insure the recovery of the jewels—the top priority of Millbank and Proust."

"But what about McKinley?" Zoe said.

Harrington grinned. "I had intended to contact you to see if you'd be interested in more work—following McKinley."

Jack nodded. "You were going to keep the recovery of the jewels quiet and see if McKinley's path crossed with anyone from Millbank and Proust."

"Yes. Not the best plan, but my company is most interested in recovery, not arrests. They are...reluctant to involve the police unless absolutely necessary."

Zoe's mind was racing as she went over the last twenty-four hours, rearranging what she and Jack knew. "The files with the details of the robberies, those were your notes. You weren't planning the crimes," Zoe said.

"You were reconstructing them," Jack said.

"You've seen my files?"

"Yes. We were quite motivated to find you and tracked down your private digs near the Pantheon."

"The apartment rental was a precaution. I couldn't risk anyone I worked with running across my research. Hotel rooms are just not that secure."

Zoe closed her hand around the brooch as she thought. "And the file with the list of people, that was your list of suspects. You were checking alibis." She tilted her head as she said, "But how could you suspect Jack? That doesn't make sense."

"Suspect Jack? That's absurd. He was never on my list of possibilities." Harrington looked completely perplexed.

"The page about Safe Haven with the notes about Jack. It was in the suspects file."

Harrington closed his eyes and shook his head. "I ran out of file folders. If I had any left, the Safe Haven information would have gone in its own file, but since I was out, I put it in the back of the last folder."

Zoe shook her head at Jack. "Lumped in with the suspects because of an office supply shortage. We certainly leapt to a conclusion there, didn't we?"

Harrington asked, "How did you find the apartment?"

"Luck," Jack said. "After our meeting at the Pantheon, we got turned around and had to retrace our steps. We happened to see a man who resembled you going in the building and noticed that you didn't ring the bell, but entered on your own."

"Hmm. Sloppy on my part." Harrington looked a bit miffed.

"It's hard to watch your back twenty-four/seven," Jack said.

"Well, apparently, I didn't do anything very well if the Flawless Set is gone, and the police suspect you."

"They have you pegged as the mastermind," Zoe said. "Jack and I are just your minions."

"As delightful as it is to know the police think so highly of me, I don't find it a great comfort."

Jack asked, "Why didn't you return my calls yesterday?"

"My phone didn't have service in Germany," Harrington said. "I had to get a new SIM card this morning, and I haven't listened to my voicemails yet. Today has been rather busy. Didn't you get my message?"

"What message?"

"Before I left town, I called your hotel and left a message that I couldn't meet you for lunch."

"We never saw the desk clerk that morning." Zoe cocked her head. "Do you hear a siren?"

They paused, and the distinctive alternating high then low pitch of a European emergency siren carried faintly to them.

Jack was already moving back to the car. "It might be for something completely unrelated to us."

"Maybe," Zoe said, but she followed quickly. As they moved through the trees to the white car, she handed the brooch to Harrington, and he slipped it back into the glove.

"Do you have anything in here you need?" Jack asked as he wiped down the inside of the door with the edge of his coat.

"No, everything is back at the hotel."

"Then you can ride with us. We'll take you to Garmisch so you can clear out of your hotel room."

"We can't just...leave it here." Harrington gestured at the car with the glove. "The tire tracks in the snow will lead them directly to it."

"Yes, but if you're not with it, you can't answer their questions. You're a wanted man."

Jack closed the door with his hip, wiped down the door handle, and then moved to the other side of the car and did the same thing on the driver's side. "If you stay, you'll be answering their questions from a cell for the next several hours, and I think we still have quite a bit more to discuss."

The off-key wail grew louder, grating on Zoe's nerves. "There's no time to get it turned around and back on the road, even if you did get it started. And that crumpled front end and the scratch on the side would be as good as a flashing sign, leading the police right to you."

"Not to mention the person who ran you off the road."

Harrington pocketed the glove. "Yes, I suppose that would tip them off that I had survived," he said as they hurried through the trees to the yellow car, their breaths creating little frosty clouds.

14

J ACK STARTED THE YELLOW CAR and pulled onto the road as soon as the doors closed. "Any idea why someone ran you off the road? Or who it was?"

"Not the slightest," Harrington said from the backseat. "And I thought I was so careful. I—" An ambulance, its lights flashing and siren pulsing, raced toward them on the opposite side of the road, and Harrington fell silent.

Zoe twisted around. "Looks like they're slowing down where you went off the road."

The sirens cut off, and there was a beat of silence. "Well, at least it was only an ambulance. No police car. Not yet, anyway," Zoe said.

"Yes, I'm sure they'll be along soon," Jack said. "Especially when they realize no one is in the car."

Jack's gaze lifted to the rearview mirror where he caught Harrington's gaze. "You said you were careful?"

"Not careful enough, apparently. I was more concerned about someone in Millbank and Proust discovering my interest in the thefts, so I set up my headquarters, as it were, at the rented apartment and kept all my documents there. At the hotel, we were spread out across several floors, so as long as I showed up early and was the last one up to bed at night, no one realized what I was doing. At least, at the time I didn't think anyone knew, but now... well, I must have been wrong. When I got the lead on McKinley— I heard he had a fabulous brooch in the shape of a bird—I made arrangements to come here to meet him, making sure not to use my company credit card. I took a few days of holiday time but didn't mention the trip to anyone."

"But everyone at Millbank and Proust didn't know where you'd gone," Zoe said.

"Odd. Perhaps the email didn't go through."

"That was how you notified them, email?" Jack asked.

"Yes. That's the way we normally do it."

"There should be a record of it somewhere. If it's not on a server, then it will be in your sent mail."

"Let's hope that is the case, but if things have gone as off-kilter as you say, I wouldn't be surprised to find that my email has been tampered with. I did use the company email system for that email." He sighed. "Of course, I wasn't trying to completely cover my tracks and have used my mobile phone as well as my personal credit cards." He took the back cover off his phone and pried the battery out. "A bit late, but there it is. At least they won't be able to track the signal now."

"I'm sure Alessi has already pulled your credit card charges and knows we're in Germany," Jack said.

"You mentioned him earlier. Carabinieri, you said?"

"Yes. He showed up at our hotel—was it only yesterday?" Jack looked to Zoe.

"Seems longer, doesn't it?" she said and filled Harrington in on the discovery of the planted bracelet.

"You hid it in your toiletries?"

"Well, I could tell from the conversation I overheard that it wouldn't go well for us if they found that bracelet."

"Where is it now?" Harrington asked.

"It's safe," Zoe said quickly. Apparently they'd been completely wrong about Harrington, but Zoe had learned a long time ago to never trust anyone completely—well, except for Jack. He was the exception to that rule, but there was no way she was giving up all their information to Harrington right now. Jack looked at her out of the corner of his eye, but didn't say anything.

Zoe said, "Until we get either the rest of the Flawless Set or enough evidence to take to Alessi to prove we didn't commit the theft, the bracelet stays where it is." Harrington didn't press for details.

"Tell him about the plaque," Jack said, neatly shifting the subject as they arrived in Garmisch. The lifts had closed as sunset neared, and skiers and snowboarders were returning from the slopes. Zoe told Harrington about the hollow plaque as they crawled through the stop-and-go traffic, halting every few minutes at red lights.

"I ordered that plaque myself," Harrington said. "It sat in my office for over two weeks. Anyone could have switched it for another one during that time. What puzzles me even more is, when were the jewels replaced with fakes?"

"Alessi thinks you did it when the jewels were transferred to the case on opening night," Zoe said.

"And how was I supposed to accomplish this feat?"

"Sleight of hand," Jack said as he inched the car forward. They rolled to a stop at the next intersection. The sun was almost down, and the whole town was in shadow. Lights glowed from homes and businesses, and streetlights came on with a flicker. The mountains themselves were darkening as the light faded. The peaks looked rough and forbidding against the last tinges of the pink and gold sky.

Harrington snorted. "I'm a magician now? Obviously, this Alessi has a vivid imagination."

"I think you're the only option," Zoe said, remembering the details with a sinking feeling. "You ordered the display, you coordinated the plaque and brought us in for the award, and you placed the jewels in the case."

"Hmm. Yes, even I can see that looks suspicious."

"Add in the other things that we know that we hope Alessi doesn't know, like our private meeting, and it looks even worse," Jack said. "Alessi also mentioned that the computer sensor attached to the display of the case showed the case had not been moved. Therefore, according to Alessi, the switch had to be made before the glass case was fitted in place."

"So the theft must have been discovered after I left Rome?"

"Yes, that morning. The clasp on the bracelet in the display wasn't broken."

Harrington looked out the window, but he wasn't studying the ornate harvest season mural on the side of a hotel. "Interesting that this theft is different, bolder. And, the use of reproductions doesn't fit the pattern of the other thefts. Why would the thief do that?"

Zoe turned toward the backseat. "To buy time, maybe? If the clasp hadn't broken on the bracelet, how long would it have been before the glass case was opened?"

"Most likely, the end of the exhibit."

Jack said, "But then why frame us with the hollowed-out plaque? That required planning."

"It could be a different thief," Zoe said.

"You like that theory. I seem to remember you brought that up earlier as well," Harrington said. "And you're right. There is that possibility. Or it might just be that replacing the Flawless Set with fakes was the only way to steal them unless the thief was willing to commit an aggressive smash-and-grab robbery during the exhibition. Those types of robberies have risks, risks that our thief hasn't wanted to take. But perhaps the Flawless Set itself was too much of a temptation. Normally, the Flawless Set isn't worn or displayed. It's kept locked away in an undisclosed spot, which even I couldn't discover the location of." Harrington leaned forward to point at the next cross street, but Jack already had the blinker on for the turn.

"You seem to know exactly where to go," Harrington observed.

Zoe handed him the driving directions. "We found this in the trash in your apartment rental. Brought us right to you."

"Police," Jack said as he cruised by the hotel, raising his hand to rub his eyebrow as they passed a police car parked in front of the hotel steps. Zoe slid lower in the seat, but Harrington swiveled and peered out the back window. "That's my room, top floor on the right." Zoe glanced back and saw the curtains hadn't been drawn. The interior light threw the shadows of two people moving around the room against the window.

Harrington dropped back into the seat. "They're searching my room." He looked dazed, like he had when Zoe had first opened the car door after the accident. She supposed it was one thing to hear the police suspected you, but seeing evidence of it was a whole other thing.

"What did you leave in the room? Anything important?" Jack asked.

"No." Harrington's gaze pinged back and forth across the backseat of the car. He patted his coat. "Just clothes, shave kit, that kind of thing. I have my passport on me and my money belt."

"Good." Jack made a few turns through a quiet neighborhood of stucco houses with heavy wooden balconies and high fences enclosing their front gardens. "I think we better get out of Garmisch. There are only a few roads in and out of this town. I don't think they'll set up checkpoints to look for us, but..."

"Better to get out now," Zoe said, wholeheartedly agreeing with Jack. The last thing they wanted was to be trapped in a mountain town. "I don't want to reenact the *Sound of Music* finale."

"And I thought you'd be up for a good hike."

"Not in the snow."

She reached for the map, but Jack unhesitatingly made another turn that brought them out on the same street they'd just driven into town, but now they were cruising in the opposite direction, making good time on the open road. The other side of the street, the road going into town, was clogged. Trust Jack to have already assessed the situation and know their exit strategies.

They cleared the edge of Garmisch and followed the swooping curves of the road as it mirrored the river. The accident scene came up quickly. The ambulance was parked on the side of the road, lights still flashing. They were by it in seconds, and Zoe only had an impression of people moving through the trees. Jack said, "I'd rather not have come back this way, but this is the fastest way out of the valley." As he drove, his gaze swept along the road. "I don't see any speed cameras here."

Zoe opened the map. "So no record of us going in or out of Garmisch."

Harrington had been peering through the back window at the diminishing lights of the ambulance. As he turned back to the front, Zoe saw that he had the abstracted manner of someone working out a complex problem. His gaze fell on the map. "May I see that?"

"Of course."

Jack asked, "So what do you think? Find some cheap, off the beaten path gästehaus for the night?"

"No." The map crinkled as Harrington shoved it into the front seat. "Ischgl. We have go to Ischgl. Tonight."

Gemma studied the abandoned car with its headlight buried in a tree trunk and compressed hood. Behind her, occasional traffic swished by on the road. Alessi huddled with Gustav, his contact in the German police force. On their flight to Innsbruck, Gemma had asked how the German police would react to their arrival. Alessi had flicked his hand, as if her worries amounted to nothing. "I helped Gustav with a missing altarpiece last year. He owes me."

Alessi said it as if that would solve any problems that came up. It probably would for Alessi, but she wasn't sure the welcome would stretch to her. She had waited until they were through security to text Nigel with the news she was traveling to Germany. Not that he'd have an issue with it. At least, she didn't think he would. It would be the higher-ups who might fuss.

But she'd learned one thing in her time with the Art Squad—it was best to get the ball rolling and then inform the people up-chain after the fact. Harder to stop things, that way. Nigel would understand completely. Heck, he was the one who'd taught her the technique. She knew if they succeeded in finding the Flawless Set, and either evidence of who stole the gems in the country house robberies or—even better—apprehended the criminals themselves along with the gems, no one would care about her unauthorized foray into another European country.

Of course, both those possibilities looked remote now. They had gone straight from the airport to Garmisch and toured Throckmorton's hotel room, which had contained nothing more exciting than a shaving kit and a run-of-the-mill suitcase. No hidden gems anywhere and no sign of his accomplices, Jack and Zoe Andrews.

Gustav had run their names through their databases and turned up nothing. No hotel or rental car reservations, and when Alessi checked back with his people in Rome, he was informed the Andrews' hotel room was still empty. Gustav had requested footage from the Zugspitze, but it wasn't in yet, so they couldn't even be sure Throckmorton had gone to the peak today. The ticket purchase could have been a distraction.

Alessi slapped his friend on the shoulder then came across the snow to her. He wore a fur-lined hat with earflaps, a heavy wool coat, boots, and gloves. A wool scarf was wrapped around the lower half of his face, covering his mouth and nose. "This weather —it is inhumane, is it not? So cold. I do not see how Gustav endures it." He stamped his booted feet and rubbed his gloved hands together before continuing. "It is the car that Throckmorton rented in Rome."

"Well, that's something, at least," Gemma said. "Did you notice the snow?"

Alessi shook his head. "No, there had already been too much activity for prints. The emergency crews and local police."

"But why would they go deeper into the woods?" Gemma pointed to several sets of prints that trailed away from the sight of the impact into the woods. "Looks like more than one person went that way, then doubled back."

"You think, perhaps three?"

"It's possible, isn't it?" Gemma said, squinting at the pine branches against the now dark sky as she tried different scenarios. "Perhaps the Andrews couple ambushed Throckmorton."

"You are thinking there was a falling out among the thieves? They ran him off the road and took the Flawless Set."

Gemma shrugged, uncomfortable. She'd rather deal with facts, but they were in short supply right now. "But then where is Throckmorton?" Gemma asked, acknowledging the major question her speculations raised. "He couldn't walk back to town without someone seeing him, surely? It's too far isn't?"

"Yes. And there are no homes or businesses here."

"The river...?"

Alessi raised a shoulder in a shrug that conveyed both possibility and doubt. "Gustav's men will check tomorrow during the daylight. Gustav has arranged hotel rooms for us in Garmisch for tonight. Then we can return to Roma." He used the Italian word for the city and said it with relish as if he wished he were already there.

Alessi had made it quite clear that any other location, even the stunningly beautiful German Alps were inferior to Italy in general and Rome in particular.

Alessi pointed out the trail of footprints to Gustav, who sent someone to photograph them. Then Gemma and Alessi turned and walked back through the snow to the cars with flashing lights along the side of the road. She'd already examined the interior of the crushed car and circled around the scene. There was nothing else to do except go back to the hotel room and go over her notes again.

And call Nigel with an update.

She burrowed her fists deeper in her pockets. No need to rush that call, she decided. It would be best to do a review, a thorough review, of all her notes before she called him.

15

"TONIGHT?" JACK SAID. "I THOUGHT you were meeting McKinley tomorrow night."

"Yes, but he made a comment today as we were parting that I just worked out." Harrington handed Zoe the map and stabbed at it. "After we go through Lermoos, we want this road here. It will take us to the A12." He checked his watch. "We should be there in an hour and a half or so."

"Why the rush?" Jack asked, but he'd pressed the accelerator down, and they sped along the valley floor, circling along the low foothills that skirted the Zugspitze, toward the wide valley on the Austrian side of the mountain.

Harrington hovered between the front and back seats, the lights from the dashboard accentuating the wrinkles around his eyes and mouth, creating deeper hollows and crevasses. He looked older and more worn than Zoe had ever seen him, and she wasn't sure if it was a trick of the light or if the strain was getting to him. He said, "This afternoon before we parted, McKinley said he was going to do another run down the mountain, and then he was leaving because he had to be in Ischgl tonight."

"To cover the charity ski tournament this week," Zoe said. "Maybe he has to check in tonight."

"Yes, but the important part is that he said, 'By tomorrow evening, I'll have more ice. Really flawless stuff.' " Harrington shook his head slightly, his gaze fixed on the map as he seemed to be reliving the moment. "I thought it was the typical salesman's pitch—you know, buy more from me. At the time, I discounted it, but now that I know the Flawless Set has been stolen." He frowned. "McKinley had put a little more emphasis on that word flawless. I think he was telling me that he would have the Flawless Set. I could be wrong, but..."

"*By* tomorrow?" Zoe asked. "Were those his exact words?"

"Yes."

"So he doesn't have it now, but he will have it tomorrow. Someone could be bringing the Flawless Set to him either tonight or tomorrow," Zoe said.

"It's thin," Jack said.

"I know," Harrington replied.

"But if there's the slightest chance..." Zoe said. "We have to try to find McKinley. We can shadow him, like we were doing to you, Harrington." She threw him a contrite glance.

"No need to apologize."

"Which way?" Jack asked. They'd traveled through the Lermoos valley, passed the curved church tower and the stucco buildings with their murals and snow covered roofs.

"Left at the fork," Zoe said, and it wasn't long before they merged onto the Autobahn.

"I can't believe I didn't make that connection earlier." Harrington had leaned back, and his face was now in shadow. Zoe could tell he was irritated with himself.

"Don't beat yourself up about it," Zoe said. "At the time, you didn't know the Flawless Set had been stolen."

"And when we told you, you'd just plowed into a tree trunk," Jack added. "It's no wonder you didn't make the connection right away. You were in shock."

"Still no excuse. We lost valuable time going back to the hotel."

"Where we discovered that the police are a lot closer than we thought," Zoe said.

"That's good info. We can use that," Jack said, countering Zoe's gloomy tone.

"Seems like straightforward bad news to me," Zoe said. "How can it be useful?"

"Well, if the police are on our trail, we can lead them right to McKinley."

"Let them think they're catching us, but in reality, they'll be catching McKinley," Zoe said slowly.

"He will have the rest of the jewels from the Rowan House robbery the next time we meet," Harrington said. "That was our agreement. The peacock brooch today—the ruby and diamond bracelet and the pink diamond ring tomorrow."

"Even better if we can somehow lead them to McKinley and whoever is handing over the Flawless Set. If they're meeting, that should be possible."

"That's a lot of ifs," Harrington said. "I don't like it."

"You're an insurance man. Risk averse," Jack said with a flicker of a smile. "I don't see we've got any other choice."

"Unfortunately, I agree," Harrington said. "There is one way to draw the police to McKinley at exactly the right moment. If I contact the police and tell them I'm willing to turn myself in, I'm sure they would be interested. If I coordinate so that they pick me up when I'm with McKinley that should insure that McKinley would be taken into custody as well." There were a few seconds of silence in the car. Zoe didn't like the images flashing through her mind—Harrington in handcuffs, accusations, criminal charges.

"It might take a while, but everything would be sorted out. I'd be cleared...eventually."

"Now that is a risky proposition," Jack said.

Zoe said. "Surely there's another way?"

"I'm not extremely enthusiastic about it, myself," Harrington said, but his expression was determined.

"If we can't find another way, we have to make sure that McKinley and his... accomplice are in possession of the jewels when the police show up, not us." Zoe said. "If we can find out who has been feeding McKinley the jewels, then I'm sure the police will be able to find some evidence of the thefts. Our problem is that they didn't seem to want to look beyond us for suspects. Do you still think Ms. Davray and Carlo are the best suspects?"

"There is no one else," Harrington said with a shake of his head. "No one else in the company had access to the information that was used to commit the earlier robberies."

"No one?" Jack pressed. "A temporary employee? A consultant?"

"No, we haven't had a consultant in the London office, and we don't use temps—that's one of Mr. Millbank's directives. Has to do with security. We use a hiring firm when we have an opening. They screen the applicants and send out several qualified candidates, then we make the choice from there."

"What about former employees? Any sudden resignations or transfers?"

Harrington stared out the window, studying the banks of snow that were dimly visible in the moonlight. "No, no one like that either."

"What about new employees?" Jack asked.

Harrington didn't need even a moment to consider that question and replied instantly. "No, no one of that level has been hired recently. It's a small group of people—Mrs. Davray, Carlo, and me—with access to the sensitive documents."

Zoe turned slowly to the backseat, working through a thought that had struck her. "What about a new low-level employee who works for someone high-level?"

Harrington stared at her a moment. "You don't mean—"

"If you want to know what's going on in a business, ask the boss's secretary or assistant, right?"

He collapsed back against the seat. "It is possible...yes, it is very possible."

Jack looked away from the road to Zoe. "The assistant? The flustered one?"

Zoe said, "She could have picked up all sorts of information working in your office. Does she have access to your computer? Your files?"

"Of course. An assistant's not much help, otherwise."

"So she could delete your email about your vacation, causing you to be the center of the speculation," Jack said. "What about access to the sensitive information related to the thefts?"

"She wouldn't be authorized to view that information, but if she logged in as me, she'd have access. Yes, it fits. The first theft occurred after she came to work."

Zoe shifted in her seat, turning fully to the backseat as she described the moment when she returned Amy's forgotten airline tickets to her in the taxi. "That expression, for half a second was so different from the usual confused awkwardness. That's what bothered me," Zoe said to Jack. "She looked suspicious and guarded, and...I don't know how to describe it. Tough, I guess."

"That's not how she looked at the exhibit's opening night," Jack said.

"Not words I would use to describe her, either," Harrington

said. "Tentative. Anxious. Bit ham-fisted, too. Always dropping things—that's how she presented herself at the office."

"So she would have known about the plaque?" Zoe asked.

"I had her place the order," Harrington said. "She could have ordered a second one and had it modified to hold the jewels."

Silence descended for a few moments, and Zoe almost felt Harrington adjusting to this new perspective.

"Good Lord! If she did it, she had me completely fooled. I wonder if that nervous clumsiness was an act. I felt sorry for her and went easy on her," he said, his tone outraged. "When I checked alibis, she said she was visiting her mum in East Anglia, and I took her word for it. I should have checked myself."

Harrington massaged his forehead. "Incredibly foolish on my part. Not only did I overlook a prime suspect because of her rank in the company, I made extra allowances for her because she seemed so inept."

"An act I'm sure she cultivated to gain your sympathy," Zoe said

"We don't have any proof it was her," Jack said. "There is still the possibility it was Melissa Davray or Carlo Goccetto."

"Yes," Harrington agreed faintly, but he sounded doubtful. After a moment, with his gaze on the window, he said, "I'd better jettison that brooch as soon as we're in Ischgl."

"You're not going to...throw it away, are you?" Zoe asked.

"No, I was thinking of mailing it to the board of directors at the London office. Anonymously, of course. It will take a few days to arrive, and by then, we'll hopefully have things sorted out on this end."

Zoe said, "When you use that fatalistic tone, it sounds as if you think the opposite will happen."

"I'm afraid the odds of everything working out well for us are extremely low," Harrington said.

"There you go again with the odds and the risk," Jack said.

"Can't help it, I'm afraid."

Zoe smiled at him over the seat. "Occupational hazard?"

Harrington smiled back. "Undeniably."

"Let's not get too far ahead of ourselves, with either worry or our plans," Jack said. "First, we have to find McKinley."

"Somehow, I don't think that will be too hard," Zoe said.

———

There was no mistaking the town of Ischgl. Unlike the other alpine towns they'd passed through, which were winding down for the night with quiet streets, lights blazed from Ischgl, cutting through the night. Nestled in a valley, it glowed and sparkled like a string of diamonds. Portions of the mountain were lit for night skiing and tobogganing, while the downtown area was busy with pedestrians. As they cruised through the streets, Jack said, "Not exactly a sleepy alpine village, is it?"

The buildings had the typical Alpine architecture—heavy wooden balconies and white stucco exteriors with murals aplenty, but there was an unmistakable tinge of glitz and glamor layered heavily on top of the mountain charm.

"No," Zoe said, "none of the other villages we've seen had high-end jewelry stores or quite so many bars."

"I believe it is known as a party town," Harrington said.

"Yep, the Kardashians would be right at home here," Zoe said.

They found a hostel on the outskirts of Ischgl that accepted cash from Harrington—he insisted on paying, saying he had plenty of cash. Jack had fought him on it, but Harrington had the last word. "I'm the one who dragged you into this, the least I can do is cover our lodging."

Their room had two sets of bunk beds, a pine armoire, and a sink. The bathroom was down the hall.

"Not exactly the Savoy, but no bed bugs," Harrington said as he examined the puffy duvet and pillow.

"We're lucky to get it," Jack said. "The desk clerk said almost every hotel room is sold out for the ski tournament."

Zoe claimed an upper bunk and went right to work, using the hostel's free Wi-Fi. "Hopefully we won't be in the room much." She typed in a search, clicked on a result, and leaned back in satisfaction. "There. McKinley's Twitter feed. I knew he'd have one, and he updates frequently."

"How helpful," Jack said.

"Isn't it?" Zoe scrolled through his recent tweets. "He posted all day yesterday about skiing in Garmisch. His last tweet today says, 'Just arrived in beautiful Ischgl. Can't wait to sample the nightlife!' That was twenty minutes ago. It looks like he rarely goes over an hour during the day without tweeting, so I bet he'll post something soon. In the meantime, I can do some other searches..." Zoe's voice trailed off as she typed, scanning websites for information about McKinley's role in the ski tournament. She vaguely heard Jack and Harrington discussing the need for more cell phones.

"Well, look at this." She turned the laptop around so they could see the picture, an action shot of a couple of guys running across a green field.

Harrington said, "Rugby. Amateur league, by the look of the uniform." He leaned closer and pointed to the player sprinting across the turf with the ball gripped to his side. "That's McKinley."

"Yes, it is," Zoe said. "See anyone else familiar?"

Jack reached around Harrington and touched the screen. "In the background, one of the spectators...is that Amy?"

Zoe smiled. "Yes, I think so. I tried to zoom in, but it gets too blurry to distinguish any features."

"Where did you find this?" Harrington asked.

"On a tabloid magazine's website. Since he wasn't tweeting, I decided to check the web, see what else I could find. It's from a profile the tabloid ran about him when he became host of the *Celebrity Insider*. The caption says he played on an amateur rugby team in his teens."

Zoe scrolled through the comments on the picture. "One of the comments is from 'AmyB.' She congratulates McKinley on doing better in life than he did in rugby then," Zoe's voice quickened. "She linked to her Twitter account. Oh, she posted a photo." Zoe clicked and another photo opened.

McKinley stood in the middle of this picture, his hair plastered to his sweaty forehead, his shirt streaked with grass stains, and his arm draped over Amy's shoulder. Her expression was a cocky, lopsided grin that was at odds with the timid, bumbling persona Zoe had encountered in Rome.

"She's younger," Jack said, "but that is definitely her."

"And the other person?" Harrington asked, indicating the young man on McKinley's other side. He wore the same uniform, but his looked crisp and clean. Not a grass stain in sight.

"Amy's description says, 'Terrance, Chris, and me after their big loss in the finals.'"

"Chris?" Jack asked.

"Short for Christopher. McKinley's first name," Zoe said.

Harrington sat down on a bunk. "So there is a connection between Amy and McKinley that goes back...what do you think? Four, five years?"

"At least," Zoe said.

Jack leaned against the frame of the bunk bed. "So they have a background, a history. That's good information to take to the police. Anything else interesting in *her* Twitter feed?"

"No. She hasn't updated it in months," Zoe said. "I'll keep looking. She might have a blog or an Instagram or Pinterest account."

"Okay, the more information we can get on her and McKinley the better." Jack looked to Harrington. "We better get those burner phones in case we have to separate tomorrow."

"Yes, good idea," Harrington said. He'd taken a washcloth from the shelf over the sink and was polishing the brooch. Zoe noticed that he carefully wiped each surface and then didn't touch it again with his fingers. He wrapped the brooch in the cloth and returned it to the glove. "I also need to arrange to mail this."

"I'll stay here." Zoe was already clicking her way through another search.

Jack tossed her the cell phone. "You keep this. We'll get two more." Zoe waved them out the door and went back to her computer.

Twenty minutes later, she'd discovered Amy loved boots, expensive purses, and geometric line drawings. She took a break from wading through Amy's Flickr photostream to check McKinley's Twitter account.

She tensed when she realized it had been updated, a full ten minutes earlier. McKinley was at a bar. She quickly plugged the name into the search engine and mapped it. He was only a few blocks away. Zoe checked her watch. She had no idea how long it would be before Jack and Harrington returned. If they'd gone out to buy gloves or a hat, they probably could find one in the first shop they came to. But she had a feeling that a burner cell phone would be a little bit harder to come by, considering that most of the businesses she'd seen on the way in were either ski rental stores, clothing shops, or jewelry boutiques. She couldn't wait on them. She scribbled a quick note for Jack, stuffed the cell phone in her pocket, and left.

The bar wasn't hard to find, but the minute Zoe saw it, she began to worry about how she'd locate McKinley. Crowds spilled out of the door and music pulsed through the air. Beyond the cluster of the town's snowy roofs, the lit ski runs glowed, slashes of white through the darkness. Zoe joined the line and was trying to edge her way inside, when she saw McKinley leaving. She realized she shouldn't have worried about finding him. McKinley enjoyed attention and soaked up being recognized. It took him ten minutes to work his way through the crowd outside the bar, stopping to take pictures and sign autographs. Zoe noticed he lingered with the prettiest girls, but when he finally tore himself away from his fans, Zoe was glad to see he was alone.

She loitered in the line waiting to get inside the bar until he was through the parking area. When he turned onto a bridge over a wide frozen river layered with snow except for a thin ribbon of water that cut its twisty way through the ice, Zoe set off behind him. The street had been cleared of snow, but a wet sheen coated the surface, reflecting the bright neon signs and the twinkling white lights that outlined some of the hotels and businesses.

The water swooshed by under her feet as Zoe crossed the bridge, keeping McKinley in sight. It was quieter on the other side of the bridge with fewer people about and less businesses, but it wasn't completely deserted. A tiny car bristling with skis mounted on the roof lumbered by.

Zoe was glad there was another person, a man toting a snowboard on his shoulder, striding along between her and McKinley. After the raucous atmosphere outside the bar, the silence seemed magnified, and Zoe was very aware of the cadence of her footsteps. But McKinley appeared to be unconcerned about anyone on the road with him. He pulled out his phone. Zoe could see the whitish glow of the screen. It looked like he was sending a text as he walked.

Her phone rang and she jumped. She fumbled with the unfamiliar phone for a second, and it rang again before she could find the right button.

"We're back," Jack said. "I found your note. Where are you?"

"I'm following McKinley." Zoe kept her gaze on the back of McKinley's head as she talked. He hadn't shown a flicker of interest in the loud ringtone. "He left a bar. We crossed a bridge over the river, and now we're in a more residential area."

"Do you know the name of the street?"

"Hang on, I'm passing a cross street now. Dorfstrasse."

"Okay. I'll be there in a minute."

"I'm fine. You don't need to hurry over here. I'll see where he goes, then come back to the hostel."

"You think I'm going to let you follow anyone around alone at night?"

"Why not," Zoe asked, bristling.

"Because it's dangerous. Don't get all irritated. If the situation were reversed what would you do? Sit and wait for me to come back, or come find me?"

Zoe twisted her lips to one side. He had a point.

"And what if he gets in his car and drives away?" Jack asked.

"Okay, okay. There's no way I'd sit and wait for you, but I'm sure he'll stop at one of these guesthouses. This looks like a dead-end road, so don't park our bumblebee of a car too close. It's pretty noticeable."

"Don't worry. If there's one thing I know how to do, it's keep a low profile. Besides, I left the hat behind. That should help."

"Funny. Your dislike of that hat is a little irrational. I'll call you when he stops and tell you where we are."

Faintly, Zoe heard the sound of a car engine turnover and the ding of the seat belt reminder. "No need. I'll find you," Jack said.

The road curved and split. McKinley kept to the right. Instead of the posh hotels in the center of town and the bright glow of fluorescent light from shops, the area had small two- and three-story gästehauses, bed-and-breakfast type places. Only a few streetlights cast feeble circles of light on the cars parked along the banks of snow that edged the road. A trio of young women chatting in German, their long curls bursting out from under their knit caps and floating around their shoulders, made their way up the street toward the lights and music of the town.

When McKinley reached a two-story gästehaus near the end of the road, he opened the front door, which threw a shaft of light across the cleared walk to the piles of snow. The snowboarder who had walked between McKinley and Zoe had stopped and was attaching his board to the roof rack of a car. In the moment that McKinley opened the door, light washed over the snowboarder, reflecting off the thick, dark-framed vintage glasses perched on his beaky nose. McKinley closed the door, cutting off the channel of light. As she walked on, Zoe sent a quick text to the phone number Jack had called from. Copying the gothic script painted on the building, she texted, "Gästehaus Maria."

The snowboarder slid into the car and slammed the door with a thud that resounded along the quiet street. Zoe kept her stride and passed the gästehaus, continuing until she came to a cleared driveway between it and the next building, which appeared to be a shared driveway for the two buildings. She strode up the driveway as if she had a car parked in the long lot that stretched behind both buildings. Once she was away from the street and in the shadow of the other building, she stopped, not sure what to do next.

The gästehaus was too small for her to go inside without drawing attention. If McKinley had been staying at one of the five-star places on the main road, she probably could have slipped in and followed him to his room, but there would be no inconspicuous shadowing of him inside the gästehaus. She supposed she could stay where she was loitering in the shadows, but it was awfully cold. Her nose and ears were numb, and she really, really wished she'd splurged for a pair of gloves when she had the chance. She balled her fists in her pockets and shifted back and forth as she watched the gästehaus, her breath creating clouds as she exhaled.

A flight of stairs hugged the gästehaus and opened to a terrace, which was covered in several inches of snow. Above the terrace, a continuous balcony stretched along the second story. Three glass doors opened onto the balcony. The one in the middle glowed with light. The other two were dark. She'd decided to casually meander up the street and check out the other side of the gästehaus when a light came on in the room to the right of the center door.

A shadow danced across the thin lace curtains, grew larger, then the door opened and McKinley stepped out onto the balcony. He paused to light a cigarette, then walked to the glass door next to his room and tapped.

After a moment, the door opened.

A woman's British accented voice carried clearly through the still air. "Ugh, stay out there with that thing."

"And good evening to you, too." McKinley propped his shoulder against the doorframe.

Snuggled under the feathery duvet in her hotel room, Gemma thumbed through her notes on her phone while sipping from a mug of hot cocoa. She finished off the drink and tossed her phone down with a sigh.

She was going to have to call Nigel and tell him she was in

Germany and that the extent of her discoveries were a shaving kit, suitcase, and an abandoned car. She rubbed her eyes and leaned back onto the pillows. No matter how hard she looked, there was no link between Harrington Throckmorton and the fence, Terrance Croftly.

There should be something. With all the research she'd done on Croftly, she couldn't find a single reference to Throckmorton. And, Throckmorton's extremely detailed files on the country home robberies didn't have one mention of Croftly. Odd, that bit, that there were no notes on what he planned to do with the gems. After reading his extensive scribblings about the robberies, she almost expected to find a list of stolen gems with notations on possible fences and value amounts. If he kept detailed notes on everything else, then why not on the disposal of the gems? Of course, it could be that he kept that information on him and not in the apartment, which would explain its absence.

A few other things about the situation bothered her. If Throckmorton double-crossed his partners, the Andrews couple, and set them up to take the fall for him, why would Throckmorton blithely rent a car in his own name when he left Rome, leaving the police an easy trail to follow? Was he so confident that the theft would be pinned on the Andrews couple? Wouldn't he realize speculation would extend to him as well?

And where *were* Jack and Zoe Andrews? It was easy to understand why they'd disappeared. Alessi had made it clear they were primary suspects. If they were smart enough to vanish without leaving a trace, why hadn't Throckmorton done the same thing?

She picked up her phone again, but this time went to Facebook. Time for a break with some mindless social media. She responded to a friend request and scrolled through her news feed. She was checking out her friend Liz's photos of a new chair she'd bought for her townhouse when something clicked in her brain.

Gemma sat up straight, as the hazy impression of familiarity she'd had earlier when she looked at the list of attendees at the exhibit opening suddenly came into focus. She knew where she'd seen one of those names before—during a search of Croftly's social media accounts. She pulled up Croftly's Facebook page and went to his friends list. "Bingo," she murmured.

She threw off the duvet and lunged for the room's phone. She dialed Alessi's number. When he answered, she said, "What do you have on Amy Beck?"

16

M CKINLEY HAD BLOCKED ZOE'S VIEW into the room when the door opened. By the time he shifted to lean against the doorframe, the woman had withdrawn out of Zoe's line of vision. Zoe couldn't be absolutely sure without seeing her, but the voice sounded young, more like Amy Beck than Mrs. Davray.

The female voice continued, the words more muted, but still distinguishable. "You're late."

McKinley took a long drag on the cigarette before replying. "I knocked on your door this afternoon as soon as I checked in. No answer."

"You're late."

"This wasn't part of the plan. I got here as soon as I could."

"I know. You had a pressing engagement with a ski run in Germany. You really should remember that your Twitter feed is public."

McKinley tossed the cigarette over the balcony, stepped inside the room, and closed the door. Without consciously deciding to do it, Zoe moved quickly back down the driveway and along the cleared path to the gästehaus. If she could find out for sure who was in the room with McKinley, at least see her, maybe get a picture, it would help them when they went to the police.

She skirted the building to the staircase, which was deep with snow. The terrace wasn't in use during the cold weather, so the steps hadn't been cleared. She dashed up them, her feet crunching loudly through the iced-over snow. The sound seemed to carry across the valley.

The portion of the terrace against the building and directly under the balcony had less snow, so Zoe walked along, hugging the wall in relative silence. She passed directly under the room where McKinley and the woman were and continued until she came to the edge of the terrace. A white iron fence enclosed the terrace and connected directly to the building. Zoe looked overhead, trying to judge the distance between the top of the fence and the balcony. It looked doable. Maybe a bit of a stretch, but doable.

Before she allowed herself to think about it anymore, she glanced around as she dusted a layer of snow off the bannister. A dog barked sharply in the distance while a car hummed along the street, but the back of the building was inky dark and deserted. The only thing beyond the parking area behind the building was the steep and heavily forested rise of the mountain. A few houses dotted a lonely road that twisted away among the trees, but it was fairly quiet. During the day, the view would be stunning.

Zoe hopped onto the railing and carefully stood up, bracing her hand against the rough stucco wall for balance. She swiveled so that she was facing the terrace then swept her hand over her head. Her fingertips brushed wood. Okay, so more than a stretch, but only about two inches.

She blew out a breath and hopped. Her hands dislodged a fine layer of snow as she gripped the lower edge of the balcony. She hung there for a moment, her heartbeat thudding in her ears, her bare fingers digging into the grooves of the wood. After another calming breath, she swung one leg out, braced her foot against the wall and levered herself up until she could transfer her grip to the decorative cutouts in the balustrade. In a few seconds, she was over the railing, the wood creaking and groaning as she transferred her weight.

She crouched low, hunkered down against the railing, the rough wood rubbing against the fabric of her coat with every breath. She wasn't sure what she would have done if someone had come to investigate the noise. She certainly didn't want to go back down, and the balcony didn't go all the way around the building. It ran across the back of the building and ended at the far side in a dead end.

But no one opened a door, and now that Zoe was on this level, she could hear the murmur of voices, so she slowly unfurled herself and inched along the balcony. She stopped short of the light pouring out of the middle room. She couldn't see the whole room, but she didn't need to. Amy perched on the edge of one of two single beds, her arms crossed and her chin down, a thunderous look on her face as she watched McKinley stroll around the other single bed.

Zoe subsided a few inches further back into the darkness as she pulled out the phone. She wasted valuable seconds making sure the phone sounds were silenced and then flicked through the features until she found the camera. She inched forward and took several pictures.

She thought they were arguing and wished she had the ability to record them, but the closed door muted their voices so much that they wouldn't be distinguishable. Zoe could barely hear them. Zoe scuttled from the balustrade to the wall of the building and eased as close to the door as she dared. She couldn't see Amy, but she could see a portion of the other bed. McKinley dropped onto it, wiggled the pillow into position behind his back, and crossed his ankles.

Amy's raised, angry voice carried through the door. "Where is it?"

McKinley's languid tones were harder to make out, but Zoe thought he said, "What do you mean, darling?"

"Don't 'darling' me. I'm not one of your star-struck fans. I've known you since we were five. You can't charm or dazzle me. I can't believe you convinced Terrance to send you the Rowen House stuff. That's not how we agreed to do things."

McKinley shrugged. "If it works better, I don't see why—"

"So let's try it again," she said, her words cutting across his. "Since you've changed things up, where is my money from this new scheme?"

McKinley extracted a cigarette, but didn't light it. "It's too soon to have anything."

Amy moved and came into view as she leaned forward. "Terence says you've completed the first part of the deal."

McKinley studied the tip of the cigarette. "Ganging up on me?"

"No, protecting my interests, our interests."

"Our?" McKinley asked.

"Mine and Terrance's. Come on, hand it over, then."

McKinley exhaled again and pulled something out of his pocket. He tossed it to Amy, and, Zoe, forgetting for a moment she needed to stay hidden, shifted forward to see better. It was Harrington's leather glove. Amy frowned at McKinley.

"Go on. Look inside." McKinley gestured, making a circular motion.

Amy pulled out a thick stack of euros and fanned the edge. Her eyebrows wrinkled into a frown. "This is more..."

"Than you expected? Yes. It's a better way to do things," McKinley said, "That's a fraction of what we can get."

"No. No new ways. We go about it just as we agreed," Amy said, but the slow, cadence of her speech was at odds with her words.

"Now, why would you say that? There's a better way than recutting the stones. We sell them to someone who wants them as is and is willing to pay a higher price than we could get the other way."

Zoe watched Amy, who seemed mesmerized by the money. She stared at it, running her thumb over the edge of the bills.

McKinley swung his feet around so that he was facing her, knee to knee. He covered her hands with his. "This way, we don't have to involve...others. Just us. That's all we need. We do this last deal and get out of here. If the gems are anything like you've said, we'll be set."

Amy looked up. "What about Terrance? We just...cut him out? Leave him?"

"He was never the essential player in this scheme."

"But we agreed. We promised each other."

McKinley shrugged and stood. "Yes, you're right. Can't go back on our word." McKinley turned toward the door. Zoe realized she'd leaned into his view. If he looked directly at the door, he'd see her face plastered to the glass. She wanted to jerk backward but couldn't move a muscle.

But he didn't look her way, only swung around the end of the bed and paced to the corner of the room where he yanked out a chair from a desk and sat down. Once seated, he was out of Zoe's view. Amy stared at McKinley, her eyes narrowed. While she focused on him, Zoe inched backward into the shadow.

"You'd do it, wouldn't you?" Amy asked.

"Do what?"

"Cut out Terrance."

McKinley chuckled. "Of course not. It was only a joke. Okay, so you've got your money, where are the new stones?"

Amy watched him a moment before she said, "I'll bring them to you tomorrow."

"Why not now?"

"Because I'm tired. And that would be breaking our agreement—always in public."

Zoe thought McKinley sounded reluctant as he said, "Always the agreement. I had no idea you were so rule bound. Okay, where?"

"On the mountain at Idalp. Meet me on the terrace of the outdoor café area at noon."

"Fine." He stood and moved toward the door.

Zoe scrambled backward, slammed into something solid. A hand clamped over her mouth.

"So it's not just Throckmorton and the Andrews couple," Gemma said into the phone as she lifted her suitcase into the trunk of their rental car. "I think Amy Beck is in on it, too. She has to be. It would be too much of a coincidence for her to know Terrance Croftly *and* work for Harrington Throckmorton *and* be in Rome when the Flawless Set was stolen."

"Yes, that is a few too many connections for my taste," Nigel replied. "So what are you doing now?"

"I'm going to Austria. Alessi ran a check of Amy Beck's credit cards—he didn't want to. It's late, but I convinced him to get his friend Gustav to do it. Amy Beck paid for a room at a ski resort about two hours from here. I don't know if Alessi is coming. He wants to wait until the morning, but Amy has been there for two days. I want to be there, if she checks out in the morning. She could be our link to Throckmorton and the Andrews couple."

Gemma slid into the driver's seat as Nigel said, "Well, I'll give you a few hours tomorrow morning before I pass the news up the chain that you're in Austria."

"Do the higher-ups know I'm in Germany?" The car had been idling and now that the heater was warm, she switched the fan to high and closed the car door. While her coat from London was adequate for any rain, drizzle, or even sleet, it wasn't quite warm enough for the Alps.

"It's on the agenda for tomorrow's meeting."

"Tricky," Gemma said with a smile.

"Just try not to go anywhere else, okay? You're already three countries over the limit."

"I'll do my best. Oh, it looks like Alessi is going to join me after all. I'll call you from Austria."

The passenger door opened and Alessi, enveloped in his layers, dropped into the seat, mumbling, "Germany, Austria. These criminals, they are crazy. Why could they not go somewhere warm?"

17

Z OE WAS SO SHOCKED THAT it took her a moment to respond. For a nanosecond, she thought it was Jack—he had said he'd find her—but she instantly realized it wasn't him. The size of the man—somehow she knew it was a man—was wrong, and a faint smell of bubble gum mixed with cigarette odor had engulfed her before a gloved hand closed over her mouth. The thoughts raced through her mind in seconds, but he took advantage of her momentary hesitation. By the time she struggled, she had been lifted off her feet and pulled back around the corner to the portion of the balcony that ran along the back of the gästehaus.

She kicked out, but her feet only thrashed against air. She twisted and writhed, but the hand remained firmly braced over her mouth. She clawed at the hand, her fingernails scraping across the fabric of the glove. That wasn't going to work—the fabric was too slick. He continued to move backward, and they quickly passed two rooms. The lights glowing from within the rooms flickered over them, and then they plunged into the darkness between the rooms again.

Zoe stopped kicking and went limp, a dead weight. She let her legs collapse and fold beneath her like a marionette dropped in a heap. He hadn't expected that. He sucked in air as her shift in weight pulled him forward. Before he could regain his balance, she gathered herself and threw out her leg in a backward stomp. Her instep connected with his foot in a jarring impact that she felt all the way up her hip.

He yelped and grunted. She focused all the adrenaline zinging around her body into tearing herself away from him.

Suddenly his hand fell away, and cool air hit her back.

She whipped around. Jack had his hands under the guy's shoulders as he lowered him to the ground. Her attacker was out cold, his head lolling against his shoulder. Breathing hard, she leaned against the wooden balcony and wiped the back of her hand across her mouth.

As Jack checked the guy's pulse, he looked up at her over the prone form. "You okay?" he asked in a whisper, his glance straying to the rooms beyond them where the lights glowed.

"Other than scared out of my mind, yeah, I guess so." Zoe heard the quiver in her voice even as she matched Jack's quiet tones. "How did you get up here?"

He jerked his head behind him. "Ladder. I found this place from your text and saw the footprints on the terrace. When I saw where they ended, I figured you were up here, even if I couldn't see you—I know how much you love to climb." Zoe couldn't see his face very well in the darkness, but she could hear the smile in his voice. Instead of being annoyed, his teasing calmed her, brought her back to their normal world of light banter.

Jack continued, "I was about to follow you up that way, when I saw someone poking around on the other side of the building." Jack stood up, still looking at the guy sprawled across the balcony. "By the time I got around there, he'd found a ladder in a shed attached to the building and propped it up against the balcony. Once he was up, I came up behind him. He was so focused on you, he didn't hear me. Come on, we should get out of here. As fights go, that was fairly quiet, but we don't want to linger."

"No, we don't," Zoe said, thinking of the last glimpse she had of McKinley as he came toward the door to the balcony. Was he out on the balcony now? She looked over her shoulder, but the stretch of the balcony that ran along the back of the building was deserted. Either McKinley had discounted the noise, or he had gone directly from Amy's room to his own and shut the door. She certainly wasn't going back by the lighted rooms to check to see if he was tucked away in his room.

She reached for Jack's hand and stepped over the guy, then paused. "Wait. I saw him, earlier tonight, on this street." The dark, thick-rimmed glasses were askew, tilted at an odd angle over his beaked nose. "He was putting a snowboard on a car rack as I walked by when I was following McKinley. Why would he attack me?"

"No idea." Jack patted the guy's coat pockets, extracted a wallet. "Felix Wenzel." The man stirred. Jack tossed the wallet on his chest. "Let's get out of here. I don't want to hit him with the wrench again. This way," Jack said, continuing to the end of the balcony where a ladder was propped against the dead-end section of the balcony.

"That sounds like something out of Clue," Zoe said, a giddy feeling creeping over her. "Mr. Wenzel, on the balcony, with the wrench."

"Technically, it would be Mr. Andrews with the wrench, since I did the hitting," Jack said. "I'll go first and brace it for you to come down. It's not all that steady."

Zoe blew out a breath. No need to get all panicky now that

everything was over, she lectured herself, but her hands and legs continued to tremble.

Jack's dark figure reached the ground, and he softly called for her to start. She boosted herself up on the railing and twisted around. It was an aged wooden ladder—it seemed everything was made of wood in this heavily forested part of the world. The worn grain of the timber felt silky against her palms as her feet connected with the ladder. It creaked and lazily swayed an inch to the side.

She gripped the balcony railing. Jack had climbed this? With his dislike of heights? He really did love her.

The dark form on the balcony groaned and brought a hand to his head. Zoe swallowed and transferred her grip to the ladder. The old wood creaked and shifted as she flew down it, moving so quickly that Jack barely had time to step back before she reached the ground. "He's coming to," she said.

"Okay. Let me just take care of this." Now that they were actually on the snowy ground, which reflected the little light there was, Zoe could see that Jack had removed a silver adjustable wrench about twenty inches long from his pocket. He used the hem of his coat to rub it clean of fingerprints then dropped it on the ground outside the shed. He grabbed the ladder and pulled it away from the building. It teetered in the air for a second. A hand appeared at the edge of the balcony, grasping for the ladder.

"I was trying to be quiet, but it doesn't matter now," Jack said, letting the ladder fall away from the building. It landed against a tree, snapping a branch with a loud crack that echoed along the street.

A masculine voice came from above, shouting in German then called, "Halt! Stop!"

Zoe turned toward the street, but Jack grabbed her hand. "No, this way. There's cover." He pulled her toward the forest. They ran across the parking area and plunged into the fragrant stand of pines, pausing only a few seconds for their vision to adjust to the deeper darkness.

"There's a road, farther up the hill," Zoe said. "It probably goes back to the town."

Jack nodded, and they set out at a quick pace, picking their way through the trees, their knees dropping down through the snow. It was easy to figure out which way to go—up. As they worked their way up the incline, some patches of snow were deeper than others, and it wasn't long before Zoe's jeans were caked up to her knees with snow. After the first few seconds of a frantic, high-stepping sprint, they slowed. The dark figure didn't pursue them; probably because exterior lights came on and several people came out to investigate the fallen ladder.

"Amy's there. She's in one room. McKinley is next door. He went to her room, and I was able to get some pictures on the camera phone of them together."

"Ah," Jack said. "That explains your impromptu climbing. I think you've invented a new sport, urban mountaineering."

They reached the road, a strip of gray that cut through the trees. They turned in the direction of town, and Zoe told Jack about the conversation she overheard.

"How does that guy on the balcony fit in?" Jack asked. "If we hadn't seen his identification, I'd think it might have been Terrance."

"They didn't mention a Felix at all," she said slowly. "Do you suppose the ID was fake, and it was Terrance? Or maybe Terrance is a nickname?"

"Odd sort of nickname," Jack said.

"Yeah. And the way they talked about Terrance...it didn't seem like he was here with them." She shrugged. "Maybe he's here, and they don't know it. But if it was Terrance on the balcony, why attack me? Shouldn't he go after McKinley? He's the one who wanted to cut out Terrance."

Jack dipped his head in acknowledgement of Zoe's point. "In short, he's an unknown variable, and I don't like that. We've already got too many of those."

"I guess we'll just have to keep an eye out for him. See if he shows up again."

"Not the way I like to operate, but I suppose it's the only option we have. So neither one of them actually mentioned the Flawless Set?" Jack asked as they trudged along.

Zoe hadn't thought she could get any colder, but the wet fabric on her legs added a whole new dimension to her misery. She burrowed her hands into her pockets and picked up the pace. "Come on. If we don't get back to the hostel soon, I'm going to turn into an ice sculpture. No, they didn't use the word 'Flawless,' but what else could they be talking about? McKinley mentioned recutting stones, so they were definitely talking about gemstones."

"Tomorrow at noon," Jack said. "That doesn't give us much time." The road emerged from the trees and dropped down to a street with several widely spaced houses.

"I know. And Idalp. That complicates things even more."

They crossed the river and were back in the village where the nightlife was still going strong. They passed the foggy windows of a packed bar where strains of oompah music spilled out into the night along with a few revelers. "What's Idalp?" Jack asked.

"It's up the mountain, sort of the hub where most of the gondolas meet, a jumping off point to catch other lifts to the rest of the mountain. I read about it when I was looking for information about the ski tournament. You can even ski over to Switzerland."

"Great. I thought you were going to say it was a restaurant or store."

"Afraid not. It's more like the Grand Central Station of this ski area."

"Looks like we're renting skis. Do you ski?"

"Of course. It's been a while, but I'm sure it's like riding a bike. You never forget, right?"

18

S HE RETURNED FROM HER MILDLY warm shower to find Harrington seated on one of the lower bunks, his phone pressed to his ear while Jack leaned against the wall, still in his wet jeans.

"Your turn," Zoe said. Harrington covered his other ear.

Zoe hung her wet clothes over the wall radiator while watching Harrington out of the corner of her eye.

Harrington bobbed his head as he spoke into the phone. "I see. Yes, I'll wait. It is urgent. Very...um, *importante*."

Jack whispered in her ear. "I brought him up to speed."

"Who is he—" she broke off as Harrington's voice rang out.

"Ah, good of you to speak to me, Colonel."

Zoe swiveled to Jack. "He's calling *Alessi*?" she hissed. "After all we've gone through to make sure the police don't find us, he's gone and called them?"

"It's our only play, Zoe."

Harrington waved his hand at them in a cutting motion, indicating they should stop talking. Zoe fell back against the wall and rubbed her forehead.

Harrington said, "Yes, I understand you'd like to speak to me personally. I'd like that as well. I have a few things to share that I think you'll find of interest. I realize that you think I'm responsible for the theft, but I assure you I'm not. I'm ready to prove my innocence to you." Harrington paused. "How will I do that?" He glanced up at them, and Zoe could have sworn there was a twinkle of mischievousness in his eye. "Why, by helping you capture the true thieves. Yes, plural. Thieves. No, I'm afraid it is not Mr. and Mrs. Andrews. Sorry to disappoint."

After another pause, Harrington said, "While I understand how much you'd like me to turn myself in at the nearest police station and give them all the details, I think it would be more effective to show you the thieves in action. A handoff of the jewels from the thief who stole them to the person who is offering to sell them back to me. Is it possible that either you or a representative could meet me tomorrow on the mountain above Ischgl?"

Harrington raised his eyebrows. "You're that close, are you? Excellent," he said faintly. He listened then said, "Fine. Meet me at noon on the restaurant terrace at Idalp." Harrington ended the call. Zoe saw a slight tremble in his hand as he tossed the phone on the bunk.

Jack picked up the phone and removed the battery.

"How close?" Zoe asked, suddenly aware of the thin lace that only half covered the black square of the window.

"Garmisch."

"Do you think that could have been Alessi in your hotel room?" Zoe asked.

"Probably."

"Well, if he's in Garmisch, he can be here in a few hours. You have to stay here, in this room," Zoe said to Harrington. "In fact, we should all stay here. If he catches sight of one of us..."

"Harrington has to stay here. Unfortunately, you and I," Jack said with a look at Zoe, "will have to go back out."

───────────

After a long night that had been short on sleep, Zoe and Jack left the hostel before sunrise and used some of Harrington's cash to convince a ski rental shop to open early for them. They collected ski gear and snagged a parking spot on the street outside the gästehaus, where they watched for McKinley and Amy to leave for the mountain. Jack didn't want to let either McKinley or Amy out of their sight, and Zoe agreed it was the safest thing to do. The downside was it meant they had to separate because McKinley was an early bird. Suited up in a red jacket, black pants, and red ski boots, he departed for the slopes at seven-thirty.

Jack dropped a quick, cold kiss on her lips. "I'll see you up there."

"Right." Zoe matched his confident, almost breezy tone. If he could mask his worry, so could she. A few years ago, she would have looked at Jack and thought he had nothing more taxing on his mind than deciding which ski run he would take down the mountain, but now she knew that despite his easy stride and calm face, he was tense and alert.

How he managed to stay so alert and focused while looking relaxed was a true skill, Zoe decided. And how he managed to do it with only a catnap, she had no idea. After Jack exchanged his snow-soaked clothes for dry clothes the night before, he had returned to the gästehaus to make sure McKinley and Amy were in for the night. They hadn't stirred from their rooms, Jack reported when he returned to the hostel at three a.m. and dropped into his bunk.

Zoe watched him stride off in McKinley's wake, expecting Amy to follow shortly, but Amy wasn't in any hurry to get up the mountain. Zoe sat in relative warmth, having to start the car and run the heater only occasionally because her rented ski pants and coat insulated her from the frigid morning air. Jack checked in a few times when he could. Cell phone service on the mountain was spotty. He reported that McKinley was burning up the ski runs, but Jack was keeping up with him at a discreet distance.

With the clock inching toward eleven, Zoe seriously began considering a repeat of her balcony-climbing trick, just to make sure Amy hadn't given her the slip. She discarded that idea and was running through possible scenarios that would allow her to inquire about Amy at the gästehaus without giving herself away when Harrington called. He said he was about to leave for the gondola and sounded calm and resolved. He wasn't surprised that Amy wasn't eager to get to the slopes. "She never mentioned skiing or any physical activity, come to think of it," Harrington said. "Not the athletic type, I'd say."

As he finished his sentence, Amy emerged from the gästehaus with skis balanced on her shoulder. She minced down the steps awkwardly in ski boots. Since Amy was walking, Zoe left the car and followed on foot, toting her skis and poles.

Zoe kept back, drawing close only when Amy entered the nearest lift house and bought a ticket. Zoe got close enough to see which kind of ticket she bought, a single pass up and down the mountain, then bought one for herself and hurried to catch up with Amy, who'd returned to the street that wound along the river.

Zoe checked the time then whipped out her phone and called the number Jack had programmed in for Harrington's phone. The three of them had agreed that Harrington would wait until the last minute before leaving the hostel so that he would be out of sight as long as possible, but now he was positioned to cross paths with Amy.

"Are you in line?" Zoe asked the moment he answered.

"Yes."

"Amy's heading for the lift house where you are," Zoe said between white puffs of breath. The road rose sharply, and she felt the altitude.

"I can't change now. The lines are quite long," Harrington said. "I'll keep my head down."

Amy paused, maybe catching her breath or maybe for a look around. Zoe wasn't sure, so she dropped back a bit, afraid Amy would spot her, but after a few seconds, Amy plodded on. As they neared the second lift house, Zoe lost sight of her. She scanned the mass of people milling around the lower level where the restrooms and lockers were located, expecting to see Amy's lime green jacket moving in and out of the crowd, but she didn't.

Zoe hurried closer, scanning the area around the base of the building as well as the open-air staircase that folded back on itself, rising to the upper level where the lift house was located as well as the tunnel with moving walkways that transported skiers into downtown Ischgl.

Zoe twisted around, her heartbeat pulsing in her ears. How could Amy be there one moment and gone the next? Zoe raced to the stairs and climbed them as fast as she could, her skis and poles thrashing around her as she sped upward. Zoe emerged into the open area between the lift lines and the entrance to the tunnel and, as if transported there by magic, there Amy was in line for the lift. Zoe blew out a puff of foggy air. She must have lost her on the stairs. Zoe fell into step behind her, pulling her hat lower over her eyebrows. She was determined to stay close to her this time.

Gemma exchanged a glance with Alessi. They were in position on opposite sides of the terrace, and she couldn't help feeling a bit sorry for Alessi. Did Throckmorton know how much Alessi hated the cold? Was that why he'd set the meeting at an outdoor restaurant? Today, Alessi had added a second scarf and, although she wasn't sure, it looked like he had on another fleece jacket under his coat.

Since Throckmorton had set the meeting on the mountain, she'd rented a ski jacket and pants that morning as well as skis as soon as the shops opened. She and Alessi had connected with local law enforcement last night and divided the surveillance. The local Austrian team took Amy Beck while she and Alessi headed up the ski lift for the meeting with Throckmorton.

Gemma didn't like splitting the duties, but she couldn't be in both places at once, and she had to stay with Alessi to be there when Throckmorton turned himself in. *If* he turned himself in. She couldn't quite believe he would willingly walk into their waiting handcuffs. But then why else would he call Alessi?

Gemma pushed the mental questions away and focused on looking for Throckmorton in the crowd. Speculation didn't matter now. It was almost time. She blew out a breath, fighting down the energy buzz she had every time before an op. There was nothing to do but stay alert and see how it played out.

Zoe pressed her phone to her ear as she waited in line for the gondola, her skis balanced on her shoulder. "I don't like it." Her heart rate was back to normal after the scare of losing Amy. She figured Jack had enough to worry about. She wouldn't bother him with that detail.

"Skiing?" Jack's voice came over the line faintly and garbled with static as if he were on another continent instead of merely a couple of thousand feet above her on the mountain.

"No, everything else. If it doesn't go as planned..." Zoe momentarily closed her eyes and tried to push away the image of Harrington and themselves in handcuffs. "Things could go bad." She focused on Harrington, who was far ahead of her in line. Unlike the ride up the Zugspitze where there had been plenty of people simply going up for the view and the unique experience of ascending to Germany's highest peak, everyone here was decked out in ski suits, helmets, goggles, thick gloves, and carried either skis and poles or a snowboard.

Everyone except Harrington.

"We should have gotten him a ski jacket when we rented our stuff," Zoe said. Harrington's black trench coat contrasted sharply with the bright ski suits and jackets that everyone else wore. "He looks like an undertaker at a clown convention."

Jack laughed. "As long as he makes it up the mountain. I think we're okay."

"He's next in line for the gondola." Zoe scanned the line of people waiting to go up the mountain then shifted her gaze to the people milling around the large board displaying which portions of the ski area were open.

Clouds had moved in overnight, blocking out the brilliant blue sky of the previous day. The gondola cables stretched up the mountain and disappeared into thick fog. A few snowflakes drifted down.

She didn't see anyone who looked like a cop, but she assumed they would be undercover. "It doesn't *look* like anyone is following him, and Amy and I are so far back that I don't think she's spotted him." Zoe's gaze had been bobbing between Harrington at the front of the line and Amy's lime-green hood. With about a dozen people separating them, she and Amy brought up the rear of the gondola line.

"No one should be onto Harrington since we kept him shuttered in the hostel last night after he made the call."

"Yeah, well, we didn't have any choice after the call, did we?" Zoe did little side-to-side steps to keep her circulation going. Her nose and cheeks were already tingling.

"Zoe, it was Harrington's choice, not mine. And you know it's the only play we have."

Zoe pulled her hat lower over her ears and sighed. "I still don't like it."

Jack asked, "How is Amy behaving?"

"She's alone and hasn't stopped to talk to anyone. She's all decked out and ready to ski, but she seems stressed." Her look of stony concentration was quite a contrast to the people around her who were in a relaxed holiday mood.

The line moved, and Zoe inched forward in that stiff-legged, slightly bent gait that ski boots forced her to take. Her toes were pinched together, but she barely noticed the pain. Harrington stepped into the small gondola. He was with a family, a mom and dad with two kids, who were swinging their poles around in a rather dangerous imitation of a sword fight. Zoe relaxed. "Okay, his gondola cleared the platform. He's in with a family with a couple of little kids."

"Phase one, complete," Jack said.

"The only danger will be if one of those kids puts his eye out with their ski pole," Zoe said.

Jack groaned. "Looks like McKinley's going out again. Probably trying to get in one more run before he has to meet Amy. I'm going to need a major rubdown. My legs are already killing me. Got to go."

Zoe tucked the phone into her pocket. The line moved and

Amy slipped into a gondola. When her turn came, Zoe watched the people ahead of her and imitated them, stowing her skis on the outer rack of the gondola, then slipping inside. With a loud snap, the doors automatically closed before the gondola reached the end of the platform. It was a much smaller gondola than the one they had ridden in Germany. This one could hold about six people. Zoe took a seat on one of the padded seats, which was warm to the touch. Heated seats in the gondola—fancy.

The other occupants were three snowboarders who were occupied with earbuds and music players and didn't pay any attention to her. The snowboarders might be bored with the view, but Zoe wasn't so jaded that she could look away from the spectacular scenery of towering snow-covered evergreens interspersed with rocky outcroppings.

She caught a glimpse of a narrow waterfall cascading over icy black rocks. The gondola moved almost vertically up the steep mountain, whisking them up at a speed that made her ears pop. They entered the low-hanging cloud, and moisture beaded on the windows, turning the view into a hazy, white blur. It only took a few minutes to reach the top, and then there was the scramble to exit and grab her gear from the gondola, which didn't stop. It moved in a continuous circuit, slowly travelling from the side of the building where arriving passengers hopped off to the other side of the building where people ready to go down the mountain could step on. Zoe snatched her skis from the rack then joined the stream of people exiting the lift house.

The ski area was above the tree line and above the thick layer of fog enveloping the lower portion of the mountain. Even high up on the mountain it was still gray and overcast, but the clouds were high enough that Zoe could see the craggy dark mountains stretching out in all directions, each one coated with a thick layer of snow. Closer, the gondola and lift cables crisscrossed the area in a crazy patchwork of cables. In the distance, Zoe could see workers operating a scissor lift, attaching signs about the ski tournament to an inflatable archway. It looked like it was the starting point of the tournament. Zoe looked for Jack or McKinley, but didn't see them.

Despite the overcast day, Zoe found herself squinting at the vibrant whiteness of the snow. Away from the main ski runs, outcroppings of dark rock thrust through the snow, their sharp edges looking dangerous. In other places, whole ridges of the unforgiving rock pushed through banks of snow.

Zoe didn't see Harrington's dark overcoat and assumed he'd already moved into the large multi-terraced building that contained a restaurant and a ski shop where the meeting was set to take place. Amy headed for one of the smaller lifts. Zoe clicked into her skis and pushed off to follow. After a wobbly start, she found her balance and managed to glide into the line for the lift a few people behind Amy.

Zoe had been skiing—once. When she was about fourteen, one of her mom's boyfriends had taken them to Vail for a weekend. Donna had been extremely put out when she discovered that her boyfriend's idea of a weekend in the mountains involved actual skiing, not shopping in the boutiques and sipping hot toddies in front of the fire. Zoe took lessons the first day and had loved the sensation of speeding across the snow. She hadn't left the bunny slope, but she'd loved it all the same.

After that disaster of a weekend, as Donna termed it, she broke it off with her boyfriend. Zoe had never put on skis again until this morning. As the lift, this one an open-air seat with a bar across it, lofted her over the busy slopes, she felt a second of misgiving as she studied the snowy expanse through a veil of tiny flakes that sprinkled down. This was no bunny slope. Could she keep up with Amy? She shook her head, causing the passenger with her on the lift to shift farther away from her. She *had* to keep up with Amy. She couldn't let her out of her sight.

Zoe exited the lift with more of a lurch than a glide, but she made it without falling and kept her gaze fixed on the lime green jacket, which was already drifting down the wide open run in a slow serpentine. Zoe swallowed. This run was a lot steeper and longer than anything she'd ever done before. She pulled her ski goggles into place.

The patch of lime green was getting smaller, and more snowflakes were swirling down, blurring her vision. Zoe dug her poles into the ground and pushed onto the run, a queasy feeling in her stomach. It was icy at the top, and her left foot vibrated then skittered away. She hunkered down and pulled her leg back in, then realized the edge of the run was approaching way too fast. She shifted her weight and swept in a curve away from the edge back toward the center of the run. Keeping sight of Amy, she executed another turn and began to relax and enjoy the wind whipping against her cheeks and the swish of her blades across the snow. Too quickly, they arrived at the bottom of the run, which emptied out to the wide area in front of the restaurant.

Amy eased to a stop, removed her skis, and propped them on a set of angled metal bars along with several other sets of skis. Sets of the metal bars were positioned across the front of the restaurant in front of rows of wooden picnic tables. Unlike the leisurely pace she'd taken down the mountain, Amy was now hoofing it across the snow toward the entrance to the restaurant.

Zoe's attention was on Amy, and she didn't see the three pint-sized kids on skis. They swirled around her, expertly swishing across her path. Zoe instinctively drew back, which threw her off balance. Instead of gliding to a stop with a shift of her skis and a plume of snow dust, she wiped out, landing hard on her backside.

She scrambled up, extracted herself from her twisted skis, dropped them on the storage rack and hurried after Amy.

Sliding glass doors swished open to a lobby area with an entrance to the ski shop on one side, a childcare area on the other, and a set of stairs and elevator directly in front of her that led to the restrooms and lockers below ground or the upper level and the restaurant. Brightly jacketed people in ski clothes moved through the lobby and to the stairs, but Zoe didn't see a lime green jacket anywhere.

19

"NOT AGAIN," ZOE muttered under her breath. Following people was hard. She definitely needed Jack to give her some lessons on it. She was already moving toward the stairs, clip clopping as fast as she could in the ski boots. She hit the stairs and went up.

One look around the restaurant sent her spirits plunging. The place was huge. Inside, nooks and crannies of booths and tables surrounded a central buffet-style area made up of several counters serving different types of foods. Through the windows, she could see rows and rows of picnic tables lining the terrace. It was the height of the lunch rush, and every table, indoors and out, seemed to be filled.

Amy had told McKinley to meet her on the terrace, so Zoe headed that direction as she checked her watch. It was five minutes until noon, the meeting time. Snow came down hard and fast now, and a red and white awning had been extended over the picnic tables. As Zoe paused on the threshold, scanning the packed tables where row upon row of people were crammed elbow to elbow over their trays of food, a figure in lime green swept by her without a look.

Amy had come up another set of stairs. Zoe breathed a sigh of relief that Amy hadn't noticed her.

Amy moved quickly through the rows of tables toward the middle of the terrace where a group had stood to leave. She slipped into the vacated spot, her hand on a fanny pack that rested across her hips.

Zoe spotted Harrington's dark figure seated at the far end near the tall glass walls that enclosed the terrace. Hemmed in on one side by teenage snowboarders and a family with tweens on the other, Harrington calmly sipped a coffee. When their eyes locked, he raised his cup in a small salute, and then his gaze shifted to a man bundled into an incredible number of layers topped with a fur-lined hat moving directly toward Harrington. He wasn't in uniform, but as he passed, she recognized Alessi's bushy eyebrows lowered into a scowl. He was the last person she wanted to make eye contact with, and she quickly looked away, focusing instead on the person who was moving in sync with him, a statuesque woman in a white ski jacket and pants with a determined gait.

Where were Jack and McKinley? Zoe tried to ignore the tide of panic that rose in her, tightening her chest. If they weren't here, everything would fall apart. Were they late? Had McKinley realized he'd been followed?

No, Zoe pushed the thought away. Jack was good at what he did—careful and thorough. He would make sure McKinley had no idea someone was tracking him. She checked her phone, but there was no message or missed call from Jack.

Alessi was at the end of Harrington's row. As he inched his way along the narrow opening of space between the tables, the tall woman in white circled around to the other end of the row, blocking in Harrington.

Zoe had to do something. They couldn't be certain if Amy had the jewels with her. If Harrington fingered Amy as the thief, but she didn't have the jewels...Harrington would have turned himself in and he would have no way to disprove the circumstantial evidence against him.

Zoe twisted around, looking along the walls for a fire alarm—it was the only thing that she could think of that would create enough confusion to give Harrington a chance to clear out. But she didn't see any fire alarms. She scooted along the wall and ran into a solid chest. Arms steadied her, and she looked up into Jack's face. "Where have you been? Is McKinley here? Why didn't you call me?"

"No time," Jack said. "Believe me, I would have knocked off a lot earlier if it had been up to me. I may not walk for days. McKinley is a skiing fiend. He just now came in." Jack looked pointedly over her shoulder. Zoe swiveled and saw McKinley breezing toward Amy, a beer in hand. He wedged himself into the bench seat across the table from her.

"Harrington's here?" Jack asked.

"Yes. Over there. Alessi is working his way through the crowd to him. There's a woman, too, at the end of the row. Harrington is blocked in."

"Only the two of them?" Jack asked.

"They came in together. There might be more police around, blending in with the crowd."

"Maybe not," Jack said. "It's not like they are trying to take down a terrorist network, just a jewel thief. There may be only the two of them."

Alessi reached Harrington, placed a hand on his shoulder, and leaned over to speak to him.

"Here we go," Jack said.

Zoe gripped Jack's arm as she looked back to Amy and McKinley. Amy removed the fanny pack, shoved it roughly across the table, and stood.

Zoe said, "It's going too fast."

"Maybe not," Jack said.

Zoe's gaze pinged back to Harrington, who spoke rapidly to Alessi while gesturing with his coffee toward Amy and McKinley. As Amy shuffled down the row between the tables, McKinley unzipped the fanny pack a few inches. Zoe couldn't see what was in the bag, but a smile crossed McKinley's face. Then he frowned, dug around in the bag, and stood abruptly, leaving his unfinished beer on the table. He spotted Amy disappearing down a set of stairs that curved down from the terrace to the open area in front of the building. He followed her.

Zoe's gaze skittered back to Alessi, who had his hand clamped securely on Harrington's shoulder.

"What is Alessi doing?" Zoe tightened her grip on Jack's arm. "They'll get away."

"Give him a second," Jack said. Alessi's eyes narrowed as he watched McKinley move quickly through the crowd. Alessi nodded at the woman, and she set off across the terrace, but someone spilled a mug of cider and several people jumped up from a table into her path. One of them, a large man, bumped into her, throwing her backward against the glass enclosure.

Jack didn't wait. He headed for the stairs. The woman regained her balance and pushed through the crowd, but instead of going after Jack and McKinley down the stairs, she headed directly for Zoe.

"Oh, good grief," Zoe muttered as she spun and dived through the crowd to the curving stairs. What good did it do to bring in the police, if they weren't going to listen? They should have gone the citizen's arrest route. At least then they would have had McKinley, Amy, and the Flawless Set. Right now they had nothing.

These thoughts flashed through Zoe's mind as she hobbled down the stairs as fast as she could in the restrictive ski boots. On ground level, she paused. The snow spun down, coating everything thickly in white.

It was more crowded than when they'd first arrived at the restaurant, and as Zoe surveyed the throngs of bundled figures zipping across the snow or flocking around outdoor tables, she felt as though she were in a busy airport the day before Thanksgiving. Then she spotted Jack running into the lift area to her right. She took off after him, her boots dragging her down and making loud thwacking sounds on the area cleared of snow around the building.

As she rounded the corner, Jack hurdled the turnstile. Inside his glass cage, a man stood and shouted.

Jack raced onto the departing gondolas. It wasn't as busy as it had been earlier at the foot of the mountain; there was no line to return to the village. The gondolas moved in their slow, continuous circuit, their doors snapping open and closed on empty gondola cars.

Zoe knew she'd never be able to hurdle the turnstile in the ski boots, so she hit the bar and pushed through as soon as the electronic chip in her lift ticket, which she'd tucked away in a pocket, activated the bar. By now the man was outside his glass cubicle, but his attention was focused on the end of the platform where Jack sprinted toward the single occupied gondola, which was slowly traveling toward the open air at the end of the platform.

There was a commotion inside the gondola. Zoe couldn't make out much at first, just limbs flailing, which set the gondola bouncing and jerking against the cables.

As Zoe pounded closer, she could see Amy's flyaway brown hair and a swath of lime green fabric pressed against the window. McKinley loomed over her, his arms extended, hands clasped at her neck. He was shouting at her, his face flushed and furious, but the glass muffled his voice, and Zoe couldn't make out his words.

Jack reached the gondola and slipped inside before the doors closed. He fell on McKinley, brought his hands down on his shoulders, and yanked him backward off Amy. She slid down below the seat, out of view.

Zoe was only a few paces away from the gondola, but couldn't close the distance. It cleared the end of the building and swung away, jouncing on the cable as McKinley lunged for Jack.

A hand locked onto Zoe's shoulder and spun her back from the edge of the building where a net extended out a few feet beyond the platform, flickering in the light breeze.

"Oh, no you don't," the woman said.

"What are you doing?" Zoe tried to twist away, but the woman held firm. Zoe pointed to the gondola, now swaying in an alarming arc. The cables groaned. "*That's* who you want—Christopher McKinley and Amy Beck."

The woman ignored her, as well as the man from the glass cubicle, who was yelling in German and gesturing at them.

Rocking wildly, the gondola moved away from the building on the gentle rise of the cable as it tracked over a road to the next support tower. McKinley threw a punch, snapping Jack's head back. He stumbled against one of the seats, and the gondola pitched like a rowboat thrown by a wave. The machinery over Zoe's head screeched as Jack jumped up, and the gondola swung the other direction as he charged back toward McKinley.

The wild swings of the gondola caught the attention of the man from the cubicle, who fell silent, and the tall woman stopped trying to manhandle Zoe back against the wall.

As the gondola tilted back and forth on the cable, the double doors separated. Amy, her lime green coat standing out bright against the gray clouds and swirling snow, peered down as she clutched the side of one of the doors. By now, the gondola was several stories above the ground. Zoe tensed, a sick feeling twisting her insides.

The man from the cubicle muttered in German what was either a curse or a prayer and ran back to the front of the lift house.

Amy hesitated and seemed to decide it was too risky because she leaned back in, but the next moment her chest pushed forward and her arms flew back. A flash of a red ski boot showed as it connected with Amy's back, propelling her out of the gondola.

It happened so quickly that she didn't even scream, just plummeted down to a ridge of banked snow around the support pole. Zoe wanted to look away, but couldn't.

Dimly, Zoe was aware of shouts, a warning bell clanging, and the machinery grinding to a halt, leaving the still rocking gondola suspended in the air above Amy, its doors now closed, a foot or two short of the support tower.

Zoe realized her hand was clamped across her mouth and that the tall woman beside her stood in a similar posture. Her grip on Zoe's shoulder had loosened, and her gaze was locked on the imprint of sunken snow where Amy had landed.

A skier swished up to the rise of snow and shouted. A lime-colored arm shifted, setting off a cascade of snow. More skiers arrived and the cadence of the voices, excited and urgent, indicated it wasn't a tragedy.

Above Amy, the arcs of the gondola were diminishing, like a pendulum on a clock that was winding down. The lack of movement sent Zoe's pulse skittering. What was going on? It was too far away to see more than an outline of a figure moving in the gondola.

Only one figure.

The doors were shoved opened again. Zoe knew it was

McKinley because of the red jacket and ski boots. He gripped the railing that ran along the roof of the gondola and began to pull himself up.

The tall woman muttered, "He's not going to..."

Oh yes he was. He was going to try to get on the roof of the gondola, and use the cable to get to the support tower, which had a ladder running down the central pole. Zoe waited a second, hoping to see Jack emerge from the car as well. There was no way he'd stay inside and let McKinley scramble over to the support tower. He didn't like heights, but Zoe knew he'd never cower in the gondola when he could prevent McKinley from getting away, especially after McKinley had shoved Amy out of the gondola. No, the only way Jack would let McKinley leave the gondola was if he couldn't stop him.

Zoe turned and ran.

20

S HE DIDN'T STOP TO CONSIDER the absurdity of running toward the gondola. If she had been thinking clearly, she probably would have stayed on the platform and done her best to convince the operator to reverse the cable once McKinley was clear.

But she didn't think. She turned and ran, pausing only to scramble over the barrier. She heard the tall woman screaming at her, but Zoe pressed quickly through the people milling around outside the restaurant and lift house then crossed the open stretch to the base of the support tower. McKinley perched atop the cable car, high above her head with the doors to the gondola standing open below him. Either the doors were broken, or the stop of the lift had disabled them, because they hadn't snapped back into place as they had after Amy fell.

There was still no sign of Jack.

The group around Amy, which was only a few feet away, had grown. Now medical people were attending to her, and most of the bystanders who'd come to see what had happened to her had transferred their attention to McKinley's impromptu high wire act.

A single long arm connected the gondola car to the cable, and McKinley had embraced it like a lover as he extended his free hand for the cable. A chorus of gasps sounded around Zoe as the spectators realized what McKinley was about to do.

It wasn't far to the support tower. Wheels that moved the cable extended out from the support column and several sections of metal ran alongside the wheels. If McKinley could reach the metal, he could move along those sections like a kid swinging along monkey bars on a playground. Within a few swings, the central pole with the ladder would be within reach—well, within a long reach—but if he made it that far, Zoe was sure he'd make it to the ladder.

She felt as if she had cotton stuffed in her ears. People shouted and milled around, but she couldn't hear anything distinctly. Her intense focus on those open gondola doors made everything else fuzzy and faint. She searched for movement inside the gondola, but didn't see anything.

McKinley straightened, released the support arm of the gondola, and transferred both hands to the cable. Zoe had seen him move lightning fast when he left the restaurant, but the height had slowed him down and his movements were methodical and slow as if someone had hit the slow motion button.

McKinley inched his hands along the cable and the gondola rocked. At first, Zoe thought it was because of McKinley's shift in weight, but then it happened again, when McKinley wasn't moving.

"Jack," Zoe breathed and wasn't at all surprised when he appeared between the open doors. He looked down. People shouted and pointed.

If the scene had been moving in slow motion before, it suddenly skipped into fast forward. McKinley saw his chance and moved back to the support arm attached to the gondola. He raised his red-booted foot and stomped down, aiming for Jack's head, intending to send him sprawling out of the gondola like Amy.

But the shouts and pointing must have clued in Jack enough that he realized something was wrong, or his instinctive dislike of heights kicked in. He ducked backward. McKinley's foot sailed down and, without Jack's head there to connect with and stop it as he expected, it continued onward, pulling McKinley off balance. He flailed, lost his grip, and fell.

Jack reached out, caught a bit of his jacket, and McKinley jerked to a stop to the accompaniment of a chorus of gasps from around Zoe.

Zoe was beyond gasping. She was barely breathing as she watched the fabric strain against Jack's fingers. Jack had both feet braced against the open doors of the gondola, which had tipped to the side because of their weight. McKinley's red boots twitched and windmilled as he dangled.

Jack's calm and only slightly strained voice drifted down. "Your hand. Give me your hand."

McKinley reached one arm upward. As their fingers connected, the fabric ripped and an object plunged to the ground. Zoe didn't even have time to jump back before something small and black hit the snow near her feet.

The tall woman—Zoe hadn't even realized she'd followed her —picked it up. It was the fanny pack that Amy had given to McKinley.

Jack now had a solid grip on McKinley's wrist, and, unbelievably, they seemed to be having a conversation. McKinley said something indistinguishable.

Jack shouted, "Any police officers down there?"

The tall woman shouted back. "Yes. We'll get you down as soon as we can."

Jack ignored the reassurances. "I thought there would be. Okay, go ahead."

There was a second's pause. Zoe squinted against the swirling flakes. McKinley's face almost looked sulky. Then Jack shifted a bit, and McKinley dipped an inch, which erased that look from his face. "Okay," he said to Jack, then looked down. "Amy did it."

Instinctively, Zoe looked to the hubbub around Amy. Medics gently placed her on a flat board. Her eyes were closed. If she heard McKinley's accusation, she didn't react. Zoe supposed Amy was probably in pain and in shock and the least of her worries was what McKinley was saying.

McKinley continued, "Amy Beck. She took the Flawless Set and framed that insurance guy and the couple."

Zoe spared a quick glance at the policewoman. She had unzipped the bag. She didn't pull anything out, but Zoe caught the sparkle and flash of gems. She noticed Zoe's attention and yanked the zipper closed.

At a few murmurs from Jack, McKinley added, "Jack and Zoe Andrews. They had nothing to do with it."

After McKinley shouted his confession, a scissor lift lumbered onto the scene. The snow was deep, and it got stuck, but it did manage to get close enough so that, first McKinley, and then Jack were able to climb in and be lowered to the ground.

Once Jack was down, Zoe sailed into his arms, noticing one eye was swollen shut and the corner of his mouth was bleeding. She wrapped her arms around him as tightly as she could. "That was insane. I was terrified."

He rubbed his cheek against her hair. "So was I. Well, I would have been if I'd been able to think about it for a moment. Things happened fast."

"Not on the ground, they didn't. It felt like you were hanging there forever."

A discreet cough sounded. "You must come with me, please."

Zoe recognized the speaker instantly. His thick-framed glasses and hooked nose were unmistakable, the man from the balcony. Jack had knocked this guy unconscious. Felix something. Had he tracked them down? Was he about to throw a punch at Jack's unswollen eye? But that was absurd. Jack had been behind this guy when Jack smashed him on the head—he had never seen Jack. And he didn't look as if he was bent on revenge. In fact, he looked slightly embarrassed at interrupting them.

They both hesitated, and the man said in his heavily German-accent English, "Please. It is," he paused, working to find the words, "official business."

Zoe could almost see Jack put on his all-business mode. "We'd like to speak with Colonel Alessi," he said.

"We know he's here. We saw him earlier," Zoe added.

The man inclined his head. "Of course."

"You can arrange that?" Zoe asked.

"Assuredly. He has worked closely with us on this matter." The man's gaze strayed to the scissor lift and the empty gondola overhead.

"Us?" Jack asked.

"The Criminal Intelligence Service of Austria. This way, please."

He escorted Zoe and Jack to the offices of the ski area management company, which the police officials had obviously commandeered. Large maps of the ski area as well as a white board filled with incomprehensible lists in German hung on the walls around the long table. He said he would return shortly.

"Where do you think Harrington is?" Zoe asked.

"Probably in a room down the hall. They'll want to keep us separate, see if our stories match up."

Zoe swiveled in her chair nervously. After the heightened reality of the last few hours, she was returning to normal, noticing that her pinched toes pained her and that her lips were chapped, miniscule details that the dramatic events had blocked out but were now coming back into focus. "Do you think that door is locked?"

"Ready to make a run for it?" Jack asked.

"You know me well," Zoe said lightly, but she was itching to get out of the room and down the mountain. "I'd rather get out of here, but I know we have to sort this out." She sighed and forced herself to lean back in the chair. "So, Felix is with the Austrian police."

Jack moved the cold pack one of the medics had given him to a different position on his eye. "Better not to mention I was the one who brained him, I think."

"I agree, but I was thinking more about how it puts a new spin on everything."

"It does indeed. Felix said Alessi was working with 'us,' the Austrian police."

"And the tall policewoman with Alessi sounds American. So it looks like we have Italian, Austrian, and U.S. law enforcement...a cooperative investigation."

"Appears so." Jack tipped his head to nod in agreement, but checked the movement and winced. "Interpol, maybe."

The door whipped open and the tall policewoman entered, her ski pants making a swishing sound as she came into the room. She had removed her white ski jacket, which revealed a white turtle-neck and a shiny police badge. Zoe hadn't seen her since the moment McKinley stepped off the scissor lift. She had grabbed his arm in her crushing grip and carted him away.

She tossed the fanny pack on the table, and the jewels partially spilled out, clattering against the table. Zoe knew diamonds were one of the hardest substances on earth, but the way the woman was handling them seemed especially cavalier. "I'm Detective Neely from Scotland Yard. Colonel Alessi you already know. Detective Felix Wenzel is from the Austrian police," she said as the men took seats across the table. So, Zoe thought, no Americans were involved, but there was definitely some international cooperation going on.

"Mrs. Andrews and I have met," Wenzel said, with a steady, almost warning gaze at Zoe. "Briefly."

Zoe got it. He remembered her from the balcony and was reluctant to broadcast the fact that he'd been knocked unconscious. "Yes," Zoe said. "Very briefly."

Neely noticed the exchange but didn't ask about it. Instead, she said, "My colleagues have asked me to lead this..." Zoe realized she was about to say interrogation, but changed her mind and finished with, "session because I speak English. They may have additional questions for you later. Now, I suggest you start talking."

Zoe felt her palms go sweaty. This wasn't the friendly chat she'd expected where she and Jack could explain what had happened. Alessi's face mirrored Neely's impassive expression. Only Wenzel's face had a hint of approachability, but the language barrier would clearly be a factor.

Jack put the cold pack on the table. "This seems a little confrontational, considering that McKinley told you we weren't involved."

"McKinley said that under duress. He's not talking now, so I suggest you take advantage of the opportunity and get on our good side."

"We aren't involved in this," Zoe said. "Well, we've been dragged into it, but we didn't steal anything. Amy committed the thefts and set up Harrington as well as us to take the blame. She said that to McKinley." Zoe looked at Wenzel. "You were there. You had to have heard her say it, too."

Behind his thick-framed glasses, Wenzel blinked rapidly, then glanced at the other investigators. Outside, Zoe had thought he was younger, but under the fluorescent lights, she could see the fine lines spraying out around his eyes and guessed he was older than she originally thought, probably in his thirties. "Yes, I can confirm," he said, carefully selecting the correct English words.

Jack leaned forward sharply. "You were investigating him, weren't you? You had McKinley under surveillance. Zoe saw you on the street earlier and—"

"Yes. That is correct." This time Wenzel managed to get his words out quickly, cutting off Jack before he could say anything about the balcony. If the Austrian police were watching McKinley, the last thing they'd want would be Zoe lurking on the balcony. No wonder Wenzel had pulled her away from McKinley's and Amy's rooms.

"So if you've had him under surveillance, you can also confirm that we—Zoe, myself, and Harrington—have had no contact with him." Jack obviously felt Wenzel was more likely to help them than the other investigators.

Wenzel touched the frame of his glasses, straightening them. "Yes, that is true...for three weeks."

Detective Neely pushed up the sleeves of her turtleneck and crossed her arms. "But you could still have been in contact with him. Through an intermediary—Amy Beck."

"We had never met her, never even seen her until the opening of the exhibit." Zoe shot a quick look at Jack. "Neither of us ever talked to her, even when we made arrangements for the trip."

"That's right," Jack said. "Harrington handled everything. I never went through his assistant. If you check, you'll find we have had no contact with her...ever."

Wenzel consulted a stack of papers he'd brought in with him. "But the five of you met at the top of the Zugspitze yesterday. Finalizing plans for the transfer?"

"No, Amy wasn't there," Zoe said. "We followed Harrington there. We were mistaken at first as well and thought Harrington had taken the Flawless Set. You see, we knew we hadn't taken it, so we assumed it had to be Harrington. We were trying to find him, so we could turn him in to prove our innocence. But then we realized he'd been framed as well. McKinley was reselling the stolen goods to the insurance company—Harrington's told you all this, right? How he's suspected an inside job and was tracking the jewels himself?" Zoe realized she was getting sidetracked and went back to her first point. "Anyway, Amy wasn't there on the Zugspitze."

Wenzel thumbed through a folder then slid several photographs across the table. The first photos showed Harrington and McKinley seated across the table from each other, the next was a shot of Zoe and Jack, also seated at one of the tables. The last photo was a wider shot of Zoe after she'd stood and moved around the open area to take pictures. Wenzel tapped a figure on the edge of the picture.

Zoe hunched over the pictures. "That is her—that's Amy." Zoe turned to Jack. "She was there. She saw Harrington. She's the one who ran him off the road. It had to be her. McKinley had deviated from their plan—he said that to Amy that night—you must have heard that, too," Zoe said, switching back to Wenzel. "Amy was checking up on McKinley. It wouldn't be hard to find out where he was. McKinley was always sending tweets. He posted several about skiing on the Zugspitze that day. If she was here in Ischgl, it would only take her around two hours to get over to the Zugspitze. When she saw Harrington, she panicked. She assumed he'd be back in Rome in custody, not recovering stolen gems. Tell me, has she been driving a gray hatchback? Because that's the car that forced Harrington off the road right after he left the meeting with McKinley."

Wenzel blinked rapidly, shuffled more papers, and then lifted his head. "Yes. Gray Renault hatchback rented in Rome." Zoe could tell from his face that he was beginning to believe them.

Neely and Alessi weren't convinced. "If your..." Alessi waved a hand in the air like a magician preparing to conjure a rabbit from a hat, "...story is true, then where is the Flawless Set?"

"Right here." Zoe pointed to the diamonds tumbling out of the unzipped fanny pack. "They fell out of McKinley's pocket. Amy gave them to him on the terrace."

"No," Neely said. "Those are imitations."

21

W ITHOUT PAUSING TO THINK WHETHER the investigators would like it or not, Zoe pulled the stones toward her. "That can't be right. I saw her give them to him myself."

The gems sparkled and glinted under the harsh fluorescent light as Zoe spread them out. At first glance, they looked like the Flawless Set to her. The stones were the right shape and size, and they certainly looked dazzling, their facets cutting the light into a rainbow of color.

As she untangled the last of the diamonds, she caught her breath. It was the bracelet. Jack reached out and took the strand of diamonds pooled in her palm. As he held it up in the air, he glanced from the bracelet to Zoe. She noticed the detail the same time he did, and it took everything she had to keep her expression from changing.

Jack touched the clasp on the dangling bracelet. "It's not broken. That's how you know they're fake?"

"Yes, that and the fact that we had an expert look at them," Neely said.

Jack raised his eyebrows. Neely shrugged one shoulder. "We have one on call to verify anything we found…"

Anything they found on Harrington, Zoe mentally added. They expected to take in Harrington and any gems he had with him.

Zoe watched as Jack lined up the bracelet, the necklace, and the earrings on the table, but her thoughts had shifted back to what she'd overheard on the balcony. "She switched them," Zoe muttered to herself.

"What did you say," Neely asked sharply.

Zoe looked from the jewelry to the three faces across the table. "Of course she switched the real jewels for fakes. I bet she decided to make the change after she saw McKinley meet with Harrington at the Zugspitze. She couldn't have McKinley returning the jewels to Harrington. It was too risky for her. I'm sure McKinley thought he could keep Harrington from ever finding out his source for the jewels, but Amy would have been afraid he'd slip up and betray her."

"So she did what? Ran out and had a copy made?" Neely asked.

"Yes," Zoe said. "I'm sure she told the jeweler she wanted a replica. And she wouldn't have had to go to a big city to get it done. Plenty of high-end jewelers in Ischgl." Zoe scooted her chair closer to the table and leaned forward. "It's no wonder she did it, especially after that conversation between her and McKinley. He wanted to cut out their third person in their group, some guy named Terrance. Amy was resistant. She said it went against their agreement, but McKinley tried to talk her into it, even suggested they could take the money from the Flawless Set and run away together. Now that I think about it, she seemed to be feeling him out, seeing how far he would go. She asked him if he'd do it, sell Terrance out. He said he wouldn't, that he was only joking when he suggested it, but I remember the way she looked at him. Her gaze was assessing and...distant, like she was calculating the odds of him meaning what he'd said. She must have come to the conclusion that if McKinley would betray Terrance, then he could betray her, too. I bet she planned to feed McKinley the fake gems and disappear, figuring she would have at least a few days to drop out of sight before McKinley learned about the switch. She didn't count on him knowing about the broken clasp, that it would tip him off immediately that they were fakes."

Jack said, "McKinley probably read some of the news accounts of the exhibit opening. Unlucky and rather careless of Amy. So where was she going?" Jack asked in an abrupt topic change.

Zoe realized he was trying to confirm that their speculations were on the right track, but Neely frowned, and Alessi remained stone-faced.

Wenzel blinked, which Jack seemed to pick up on as some sort of tell. Jack zeroed in on him. "South Africa? The Caribbean? Come on, you can let us in on that little detail. You were watching McKinley, and he spoke to Amy last night, so I'm sure you've run down any travel plans she had."

Wenzel retrieved the Zugspitze photographs and carefully returned them to a file folder, which he closed with an air of finality. "Belize."

Neely threw her gaze up to the ceiling and pushed away from the table.

"Excuse me." Wenzel stood, tucked the files under his arm, and turned to the investigators. "A word, please." He escorted them out of the room. They left the door open a crack, and Zoe could see them huddled in the hall.

Jack leaned back. "Wenzel believes us, and he's the important one."

"What about Neely and Alessi?"

"This is Wenzel's territory. Even if Interpol is involved, this is Austria. Wenzel makes the calls here."

"Well, I'm glad he believes us, but we need the other two on our side, too. We can't stay here forever, and I'd like the option of visiting Italy again someday."

"I think we can work out something. An exchange—" Jack broke off as the three investigators returned to the room. Wenzel moved confidently, this time taking the center seat. The sour faces of Neely and Alessi bracketed him, but they sat down. *Jack has it right*, Zoe thought. They don't like the way this is going, but Wenzel has the last word here.

"Amy Beck did have a flight booked," Wenzel said, with the air of a man getting down to important business. "Tomorrow morning from Innsbruck. Everything you say...is okay. Checks out with our knowledge on McKinley. I believe you. My colleagues are suspicious, but I believe you could be a great asset to us."

During Wenzel's labored speech, which had been peppered with many pauses as he thought of the right word, Neely had pressed her lips together. Finally, it seemed, she couldn't keep the words inside any longer. "Assets," she said, frustration lacing her words. "Sure, let's bring them in. Let's trust them. They can help us find the real Flawless Set."

Jack tilted his head, ignoring the sarcastic tone. "It wasn't in Amy's hotel room?"

"No," Neely said reluctantly.

"She wouldn't leave it there. Too vulnerable," Zoe said. "If McKinley happened to realize that she'd made a switch, the first thing he'd do would be search her room."

"No, the first thing he did was try to choke the truth out of her," Jack said. "He was shouting, 'Where is it? Where is it?' when I got on the gondola. Never mind that he wasn't giving her a chance to answer."

"We are glad you were there to intervene," Alessi said, his tone serious.

"Anyone would have done the same thing."

A faint smile crossed Alessi's face. "No, many would *not* have stepped in." Clearly he wasn't sold on the idea that Jack and Zoe weren't part of the gang of thieves, but he was giving Jack his due for trying to prevent Amy's death.

"Unless we can get Amy Beck to talk, we'll probably never find it," Neely said. "It could be anywhere from Italy to here. She had ample time to hide it or hand it off to someone."

"Did the medical people check her clothes?" Jack asked.

Neely laughed. "You think she kept it on her?"

Jack shrugged. "What was in Amy's pockets?"

Wenzel consulted his phone. "Sunglasses, balm for the lips, lift ticket, key, thirty euros, and a passport."

"Her own?" Jack asked.

"It does not say. I assume so. Otherwise, it would have been noted."

"Did you say a card key? Like a key to a hotel room?" Zoe asked suddenly.

"No, a key. Metal."

"Probably to her hotel room," Jack said. "The smaller hotel and guesthouses don't have key cards."

"Right, but in those types of places you turn in your key at the front desk at the guesthouse. Like we did at our hotel in Rome, so it's probably not a hotel key." She grinned. "I know where it is. I know where the Flawless Set is."

Jack sent her a warning look. "You mean you know where part of the Flawless Set is."

Zoe shook her head slightly, trying to indicate that she wasn't talking about the bracelet, the real bracelet that was back in Rome, which she knew Jack still considered their bargaining chip.

She sent him a reassuring smile. "No, I know where the whole thing is. We need that key."

"It has to be here," Zoe said to Harrington as they filed into the room lined with lockers. They were at the base of the ski lift, in one of the ski storage areas. Zoe had asked if Harrington could accompany them to see the locker, and Wenzel had agreed immediately.

"I would be absolutely thrilled to wrap this thing up, but why are you so sure?" Harrington asked. He looked as unflappable as ever, not a gray hair out of place and his trench coat neatly buttoned against the cold. His cheeks were ruddy, and he still had dark circles under his eyes, but his gaze sparkled with a new vitality that hadn't been there this morning.

"Because I lost Amy earlier today when we arrived here." We were outside, on the ground level. One moment she was ahead of me in the crowd and the next she'd vanished. I panicked, of course, and spent several minutes searching the crowd, then I raced up the stairs and found her waiting for the gondola." She noticed Jack was taking in her story as well.

"You didn't tell me that," he said.

"I didn't think it mattered. I'd found her again by the time I talked to you, but when Wenzel mentioned the key, I realized what had happened. She'd come in here to stash something, the Flawless Set of course—what else could it be—in a locker then she took the elevator up to the gondolas. That's why I never saw her on the stairs and how she seemed to appear out of thin air."

Jack looked around the room. "It does make sense. It was away from her hotel room, and she could retrieve it after the meeting with McKinley." The locker depot reminded Zoe a bit of her high school locker room with its tile floor and full size lockers, but instead of a plastic bench in front of the lockers, this room had rows of padded chairs.

Wenzel, Neely, and Alessi had formed a group on the opposite side of the chairs. The ski lift was running again, and it had been a crowded and tense descent with all of them packed into one gondola.

A skier closed a locker, removed the key, and left, giving both huddled groups long stares.

A man in uniform entered, went straight to Wenzel, and handed him a key. Wenzel checked the number and moved to a locker near Zoe's group. He had trouble fitting the key into the lock.

Zoe had been so sure on the way down the mountain, but now, with everyone's attention focused on the locker, doubt pricked at her. What if she was wrong? Would she have just wiped out their credibility? Jack had insisted all the investigators agree in writing that their cooperation and return of the Flawless Set would insure immunity for herself and Jack as well as Harrington.

Wenzel finally got the key into the lock. He twisted and pulled. The door fell back and Zoe felt as if she'd swallowed a rock.

It was empty. Zoe shot a panicked look at Jack. "But it should be there."

Harrington stroked his mustache and murmured, "Don't give up yet, my dear."

Instead of turning accusingly toward her as she'd expected, Wenzel was running his hands over the seams of the locker, examining the door, then the hinges, and the walls. Neely danced on either side of his shoulders, while Alessi was circling the room, examining the tops and bottoms of the lockers.

Wenzel, his head inside the locker, said something in German. Everyone crowded closer. Alessi stopped peering under the chairs and joined them. "I have found it. It is taped to the top." As he spoke, he was working, pulling at something, then it gave and a cloth-wrapped bundle thudded to the bottom of the locker. Wenzel cringed at the noise, then carefully picked up the tape-encrusted bundle. He pulled out a pocketknife—a Swiss Army knife Zoe noted distractedly—and cut an incision in the tape.

He carefully opened the slit.

Zoe hadn't realized she'd been holding her breath, and it came out in a whoosh. He used the knife blade to extract the necklace. As his hand rose in the air and the strand of diamonds emerged, flashing and sparkling, they were all silent. The diamonds were incredibly beautiful—stunning. They literally took everyone's breath away.

Wenzel peered into the bag then turned sharply to Zoe. "The earrings are here, but no bracelet."

"I said I knew where the Flawless Set was. I never said the pieces were together."

22

"I COULD GET USED TO this," Zoe said over the noise of the siren as the streets of Rome zipped by the window of the police car.

Jack looked across their coats, which were piled in the seat between them. They'd shed their coats the minute they stepped out of the airport into the balmy sunshine. It was sixty-eight degrees, but after the Alps, it felt as if they'd landed in the tropics. "I just hope this really is an escort to the bag deposit shop and not a one-way trip to the local police station."

Zoe slipped on her sandals then stowed the bulky snow boots in the floorboard. "Oh, I think Alessi will keep his word."

"Then you have more faith in the police than I do."

"No, I know Alessi wants the Flawless Set, the *complete* Flawless Set. We have the advantage."

"Until we turn over the bracelet," Jack said.

"We've got a plan. It will work. You're usually not this pessimistic."

"I know." Jack scrubbed his hand over his face. "Must be the lack of sleep. That nap on the plane didn't help much."

They had been up most of the night, repeating their story again and again to various officials. Finally, Wenzel had cleared them to leave Austria, and Zoe was sorry that he wasn't coming to Rome with them. He was their strongest ally, but she supposed that he wouldn't have as much pull in Italy as he did in Austria. Alessi had arranged for them to be on the first flight from Innsbruck to Rome the next morning, so they'd cleared out of the hostel and headed directly to the airport in the early hours of the morning, all with Alessi constantly by their side. Zoe hadn't seen Neely, the representative from Scotland Yard with the American accent, since they left the room with the lockers.

Zoe glanced out the back window at the police car behind them. Alessi was in the passenger seat. She couldn't see Harrington in the back. "I don't think we have anything to worry about. Alessi has thawed quite a bit toward us."

"You think?"

"Yes. He's not glowering at us constantly. That's an improvement. I think he might actually smile before the day is over."

The narrow streets of central Rome closed in around them as the driver navigated through the motor scooters, cars, and pedestrians clogging the roads. The driver double-parked in front of the bag deposit shop, and cut the siren, then Zoe could hear the cacophony of the city: car horns, voices, engine noise, and distant sirens.

Alessi pulled in behind them, and he and Harrington joined them on the sidewalk. Alessi said a few words to the officer who had driven them, then gestured for Zoe and Jack to precede him into the shop.

Jack checked his phone. "We need a moment," he said to Alessi while scanning the street. Alessi frowned. Jack raised his hand and a man in a dark suit and gray tie crossed the street to join them. He was young, probably in his mid-twenties. His neatly trimmed blond hair and a clean-shaven face gave him a fresh-scrubbed All-American look.

"Mark Downs, American Embassy," he said, shaking Jack's hand.

"Thank you for coming," Jack said. "My wife, Zoe." Jack proceeded to introduce him to everyone, ending with Alessi.

As Mark shook Alessi's hand, he said a few sentences in Italian. The only words Zoe caught were good morning. With a glance at Jack, Mark switched back to English, saying, "I'm only here as a formality. Just to make sure the agreements are abided by." He looked back to Alessi. "I'm sure you understand."

Alessi nodded. "Now, we proceed?"

"Yes." Jack propelled Zoe along with him through the door Alessi held open.

"Feel better now?" Zoe asked Jack.

"Immensely."

"Good. I'm glad you were able to get in touch with the embassy last night."

"It can't hurt to have a little insurance," Jack said, catching Harrington's eye as they passed the rows of washing machines on their way to the luggage storage counter at the back.

"You'll get no argument from me there," Harrington said.

"Alessi is glowering again," Zoe said with a sigh. "Well, maybe this will make him happy." The same Indian man who had helped them before stood behind the counter, looking leery as the large group approached, but when Zoe handed over the luggage ticket his face cleared. He was back within seconds, placing the suitcase on the counter. Zoe signed for it.

Jack unzipped it, and Zoe pulled out the blanket, feeling the hard lump of the lotion bottle in the middle. She and Jack exchanged a relieved look. Neither one of them had mentioned the fear that the bottle might be gone, but she knew the thought had crossed both of their minds. She unwrapped the bundle and handed the bottle to Alessi.

He scowled. "Here?"

"Yes."

He muttered something about a pink panther before spreading the blanket on the counter.

Zoe looked at Jack. "Pink Panther? Like the gang?" Zoe had heard about the group of thieves called the Pink Panther gang, who had pulled off daring, attention-getting robberies.

Jack shrugged. Alessi squeezed the bottle and dollops of lotion landed on the blanket. The man behind the counter shuffled closer, then backed away. Zoe thought he looked like he wanted to call the police, but since the police were here, creating a mess on his counter he didn't know what to do.

Harrington leaned in and said quietly, "I believe he was referring to the original Pink Panther movies. In one of them, a diamond is hidden in face cream."

"I had no idea," Zoe said. "There was nowhere else to hide it."

Alessi banged the bottle against the counter like he was hammering a nail. A string of dollops trailed out across the blanket. He dropped the bottle and used the corner of the blanket to wipe the lotion away, revealing a row of flashing diamonds. The man behind the counter gasped. Alessi's scowl disappeared.

Zoe looked at Jack. "I told you he'd smile."

Nigel crossed the room to Gemma's desk, a lidded cup of coffee in each hand. He handed one to Gemma. "Café Mocha, your favorite, I believe."

"Yes, it is. Thank you."

Nigel raised his cup to her. "Nice work on the Flawless case and the country home robberies."

She raised her cup as well. "Thanks." She looked at the folded newspaper he held clutched to his side under his elbow. "Nice photo."

Under the headline, "Flawless Find: Art Squad Recovers Famous Diamonds," were two photos, one a close-up of the Flawless Set and the other of Nigel behind a podium at the press conference.

"I'm not photogenic at all. Too much reflection," he said, rubbing his hand over his head.

"I meant the diamonds."

"Of course you did. So, what happened with Terrance Croftly? I would have liked to have been in on that interrogation, but duty called," he said raising the newspaper.

"Croftly couldn't wait to sell out McKinley and Beck," Gemma said. "He talked so much that it more than made up for their silence."

"So he admitted to receiving stolen gems and his intent to sell them?"

"Yep. He gave me the background on the scheme. He, McKinley, and Beck grew up in the same neighborhood. They went their separate ways a few years ago. Croftly went to train with his uncle, the jewel cutter. McKinley hit the big time with the celebrity gossip show host job, and Amy bounced around from job to job in London, working as a bank teller, and then a few different secretarial jobs. They stayed in touch."

"Sounds normal enough."

"It does, except that McKinley wasn't satisfied with his job or his income. Ambitious was how Croftly described it, always wanting more."

"So a job interacting with people who made pots of money for singing a song or reciting lines in a movie must have rubbed him the wrong way."

"Yes, but he didn't go outside the lines until a starlet he was dating was written out of her television show and suddenly didn't have any money to pay for her extravagant lifestyle. McKinley told Croftly it was the woman who came up with the burglary insurance scam idea. He agreed to help her stage the theft of some of her jewelry."

"Handy that he should have a jewel cutter as an old friend."

"Isn't it?" Gemma said. "They pulled it off. The insurance company paid, and she had enough to stay afloat until her next part came through."

"And a scheme was born?" Nigel asked.

Gemma nodded. "Apparently the word got out to the glitterati that if you needed cash and had some nice jewels on hand, McKinley was your man. Then Amy got the job working for Harrington and they brought her into it."

Nigel sat down on the corner of her desk. "The opportunity must have been too good to pass up—all that information on those nice gems just sitting in country homes with lax security."

"Yes, but Amy insisted on some guidelines. They each got an equal cut of the proceeds, and all their transfers had to be made in a public place. That's why she insisted on meeting in Idalp."

"Doesn't sound like she trusted her partners completely."

"With good reason," Gemma said. "McKinley planned to cut out on her and Terrance. He had a flight booked that evening to New York. I suppose he thought that if he double crossed them, they wouldn't be able to do anything."

"They certainly wouldn't be able to go to the police," Nigel said.

Gemma leaned back in her chair. "That old saying about no

honor among thieves is true. Beck and McKinley both had plans to escape alone with the Flawless Set."

"No plans like that for Croftly?"

"Not that we've found, but he's jumped at the chance to provide evidence on the other two, so he's not exactly being loyal either."

"And the gems from the country house thefts? What's the status on those?"

"All recovered. Croftly removed them from their settings, but we found them exactly where he said they would be—stashed in a carrier bag in a storage facility. It will take some work, but it looks like they'll all be able to be reset and returned, even the medieval cross."

"Excellent." Nigel tilted his head to see what was on her desk. "Ah, the Claesz, again. I think you've earned a few days to work on that. Carry on." He handed her the newspaper. "For your wall," he said and moved on to his office.

Gemma opened a drawer, pulled out a pair of scissors, and clipped the photo of the Flawless Set from the paper. She stuck a piece of tape on it and aligned it with two other clippings of paintings that were taped to the filing cabinet that edged her desk.

She sipped her coffee and studied the clippings with a feeling of intense satisfaction. Three closed cases. Three recoveries. Three recoveries were nothing compared to some of the old-timers on the Art Squad, but she'd helped recover stolen goods—priceless, beautiful items. She'd played a part in bringing them back from the seemingly bottomless pit of the black market.

She finished the coffee and swung her chair back to her desktop. "Now back to my Dutch paintings."

Harrington raised his glass across the linen-covered table. "To uncovering the thieves and recovering the Flawless Set."

Zoe and Jack touched their glasses against his. Zoe and Jack had met Harrington after the siesta at a café with a view of the Pantheon.

"Will it be back on display soon?" Jack asked.

"Tomorrow. I'm extending a few days to supervise the transition and wrap up everything with the Italian government. Then I'll be heading home."

"Just like us." Zoe glanced around the piazza with a sigh. "Not quite the Roman holiday we expected, but at least we did get to see Rome."

"With the added side-trip to the Alps," Jack said.

"True," Zoe said. "It was a one of a kind trip." She took another sip of her fizzy drink and tried to fight off the sense of impending letdown, the end-of-the-party disappointment feeling, that had crept over her as they returned to the hotel and began repacking their suitcases for their flight in the morning.

There was no travel manuscript waiting when she got back— not that she wanted more manuscripts, but at least it would be work, which would bring in some money. Being a suspect in a jewel heist had pushed thoughts about work out of her head, but now that flat feeling was creeping back.

"So what has happened with Amy and McKinley?" Jack asked, drawing her attention back to the conversation.

"Bit of an international tussle, that one. The Austrians want to charge them and of course, we—the Brits, I mean—do, too. Then there is Italy, where the theft of the Flawless Set occurred, but we now have evidence tying both of them, as well as their jeweler accomplice, to the thefts at the country houses. Once the paperwork and jurisdictions are sorted out, I believe Amy will have charges filed against her here in Italy as well as in England. She'll have to recover from her broken leg, but it's mending nicely, I'm told. McKinley will face charges in England as well as several European countries where he made his deals. The courts will sort it out. I'm afraid neither one of them will get long sentences. In the end, they were thieves. Property crime isn't punished as severely as violent crime. The bright spot is that the gems have been recovered. Croftly had only removed the gems from their settings and hadn't recut them yet, so Millbank and Proust will be able to return the gems to the owners."

"And save on hefty payouts?" Jack asked.

"Yes, indeed. The most important aspect of the whole thing in Millbank and Proust's view.

"Has anyone figured out how she did it? How she got the Flawless Set out?" Zoe asked.

"She's not talking, but Alessi told me they found emails confirming she ordered a second, hollowed-out plaque as well as copies of the Flawless Set. She also contacted a hacker and had him get into the power grid and cut the power to the palazzo as well as some of the surrounding buildings for several days leading up to the opening, creating intermittent power outages. On the night of the opening after everyone left, he cut the power to the palazzo, allowing her to get in and get into the Flawless display. Since temporary blackouts were part of a prior pattern, and there was also a thunderstorm in the area, the police discounted it.

"While the power was out, she used the codes she'd taken from my computer to open the display and switched the real diamonds for the copies. The next morning, she slipped into your hotel, took your room key while you were out, and planted the bracelet in your room. Then she raised the alarm about the switch and contacted the police with the anonymous tip about the bracelet being in your hotel room."

"So the plaque *was* a red herring," Zoe said. "I told Alessi it might be."

"She needed an explanation for how the thieves got the Flawless Set out of the exhibit that would prevent the police from looking into who would have had access after closing time. By using the plaque, she focused their attention on the wrong time," Harrington said.

"And the wrong people." Zoe shivered despite the warm night. "If all had gone according to her plan, Alessi would have found the bracelet, and we would have spent the rest of our time in Rome in some jail cell."

"Yes, but it didn't happen that way, thank goodness," Harrington said. "Oh, I almost forgot." He put down his drink and removed his phone from his pocket. "I am forwarding this letter from Mrs. Davray to your email."

Jack took the phone from him, a wary look on his face. At the mention of Mrs. Davray, all the concern about the business swept back in. The craziness in the mountains had pushed it out of Zoe's thoughts, but now the prospect of difficult times for the business came back into focus. It felt like a weight had landed on her shoulders.

Jack read a few lines then looked at Harrington. "You're sure this is from Mrs. Davray?"

"Yes. Rather frightening how quickly she has switched points of view, isn't it?"

Jack read a few lines aloud. "She says she is 'grateful for the assistance that Safe Haven has provided to Millbank and Proust, and we are once again indebted to them.' "

"Wow. And she swore we'd never do business again," Zoe said.

"Just shows how much impact a few news items can have," Harrington said.

"Thank you," Jack said.

"Not my doing. Well, not *all* my doing. The various police forces want to get their 'props,' as I believe you call it."

Zoe laughed at his exact diction as he pronounced the slang. "Well, as long as it keeps Safe Haven operating, that's a good thing."

Jack lifted his glass to Zoe. "I'm usually not one to praise the press, but in this case, I agree."

"Since we're discussing business, I have a proposition," Harrington said.

Here it comes, she thought, that offer for additional work that Jack was hoping for. The business might survive after all. Zoe scooted her chair back. "I think I'll take a last stroll around the campo, leave you two alone to talk."

"But you are the one I want to talk to."

"Me? You want to talk business with me?"

"Yes." Harrington glanced at Jack. "Of course, Millbank and Proust wants to continue our association with Safe Haven. You can see that from the tone of Mrs. Davray's letter. You were invaluable...after you stopped suspecting me, but we will gloss over that detail," he said with a quick smile. Turning to Zoe, he said, "I have a short time left with the company. After I retire, I plan to set up my own insurance investigation firm. Would you consider working with me as a recovery consultant?"

"Me?" It seemed to be the only word she could get out.

"Yes. This case and the prior one you helped out with revealed you have a unique ability. In short, you have a knack for this sort of thing—tracking things down."

"You don't know the half of it," Jack said. "She tracked me down."

"Twice," Zoe reminded him.

Harrington said, "Yes, I heard. You'll have to fill me in on the whole story someday. I'd love to hear it now, but I must finish my pitch." He leaned over the table. "You're persistent and innovative. And you have a...let's call it a unique network to gather information from."

Zoe couldn't help but smile. "That is a delicate way to phrase it," she said, thinking of all the people she'd connected with during the last few years. "Definitely sounds better than crooks, ex-hackers, and dodgy antique dealers. I'd never thought of it that way, but you're right. I do know a lot of diverse people in different areas. I even know some FBI agents and an investigative reporter."

"But you aren't in law enforcement or insurance, so you have an unusual approach, a fresh one. We often need that." Harrington leaned forward. "What do you say? Will you consider it?"

Zoe looked to Jack. "Can you believe this?"

He grinned at her. "Yes, I can. In fact, I'm not surprised at all."

Zoe scooted her chair closer to the table. "I'm in."

Jack laughed. "That's my Zoe. Never the tentative approach, always in with both feet."

"What? I love the idea, and I *am* good at finding things."

Harrington turned to Jack. "Besides recovery, I also plan to consult with businesses—museums, private individuals, that sort of thing—and provide security assessments. Preventative maintenance, if you will. Would you be interested? "

"Of course," Jack said. "But don't think it escaped me that I'm riding Zoe's coattails into this deal."

"Nonsense. I want both of you onboard—" he broke off as he caught the wink Jack sent Zoe. "Having a bit of fun with me, are you? Can't have any of that. Strictly all work, no fun in my outfit. Now, what do you say we seal this deal with a toast and go find the rest of Rome's obelisks? You have to see them all."

"Sounds wonderful," Zoe said. "Someone owes me a pizza." She lowered her chin and stared at Jack.

"That should be possible," Jack said. "We are in Rome, after all. Got to be a decent pizzeria around here somewhere."

"Excellent." Harrington raised his glass. "To our new partnership."

"Our new partnership," Zoe and Jack echoed as the three glasses clinked together.

Want to know when the next Zoe book is coming out? Sign up for Sara's updates at SaraRosett.com/signup.

A NOTE FROM THE AUTHOR

This book is for all the readers who asked for another Zoe book. Thank you for supporting the series and helping me spread the word about it. I appreciate it! As always, I'd love it if you'd post an online review or tell other readers about the series.

When I began to think about another Zoe and Jack book, I realized that in the other books in the *On the Run* series I had only mentioned Rome in passing. How could I *not* have set a book in Rome, one of my favorite cities? How could I have overlooked it? Well, that's rectified now with *Suspicious*. Zoe and Jack explore some of my favorite things about the city—the Pantheon, the obelisks, the fountains, the markets, and the food. There's so much history and so many amazing sights, I couldn't include them all, but I hope *Suspicious* gives you a taste of the Eternal City and either brings back good memories if you've traveled there or inspires you to visit someday. It's a city like no other.

Now, a few points for clarification. First, the Art Squad in London is part of the Metropolitan Police, which is also known as Scotland Yard. For consistency and ease of recognition, I used the term Scotland Yard in this story.

Second, I had to resurrect a business for the story. If you look for the laundry/bag deposit shop near the Termini, it is now closed, but it did exist at one time. If you're looking for a place to drop your luggage for a few hours in Rome, your best bet now is the Left Luggage area of the Termini, or you can try a private pick up and drop off luggage service.

For invaluable and interesting background research on art theft and art theft recovery, I read *The Rescue Artist* by Edward Dolnick and *Priceless* by Robert K. Wittman. Both are excellent reads, if you're curious about how lost art is recovered.

You can check out some of the images that inspired me and some of the places mentioned in Suspicious Pinterest page.

GET THE NEXT BOOK

Devious
Book Five in the *On The Run* Series

Free-spirited Zoe Andrews has settled into married life and feels she has found her ideal niche working for a company that discreetly recovers lost items for elite clients, but her first assignment, which takes her to Edinburgh to recover a stolen painting, turns out to be more complicated than she expected.

Instead of simply getting in touch with contacts in the art world, Zoe finds herself tangled in a web of contradictions. Why would someone steal a not-so-valuable painting, and why was the thief attacked? Zoe's search to find answers takes her from the ancient stone walls of Edinburgh Castle to the Baroque grandeur of Salzburg as she delves into a decades old mystery with ties to the present.

ABOUT THE AUTHOR

USA Today bestselling author Sara Rosett writes fun mysteries. Her books are lighthearted escapes for readers who enjoy interesting settings, quirky characters, and puzzling mysteries. "Publishers Weekly" called Sara's books, "satisfying," "well-executed," and "sparkling."

Sara loves to get new stamps in her passport and considers dark chocolate a daily requirement. Find out more at Sara-Rosett.com.

Connect with Sara
www.SaraRosett.com

OTHER BOOKS BY SARA ROSETT

This is Sara Rosett's complete library at the time of publication, but Sara has new books coming out all the time. Sign up for her updates at SaraRosett.com/signup to stay up to date on new releases.

High Society Lady Detective series

Murder at Archly Manor

Murder at Blackburn Hall

The Egyptian Antiquities Murder

Murder on Location series

Death in the English Countryside

Death in an English Cottage

Death in a Stately Home

Death in an Elegant City

Menace at the Christmas Market (novella)

Death in an English Garden

Death at an English Wedding

CPSIA information can be obtained
at www.ICGtesting.com
Printed in the USA
FSHW011954151021
85525FS